A-21

Tim Hancock

A-21

ISBN: 1484147952
ISBN-13: 9781484147955

DEDICATION

This work is dedicated too my father, who I dearly miss, my mother, who may not enjoy some of the language and to my family. Without you all I would have never had the courage.

ACKNOWLEDGMENTS

I would like to thank my wife Rhonda and daughter Kristen. Their persistent impatience for new pages drove this work to the end. I couldn't have gotten this far without their editing input. Well, it would have taken longer. Of course I would like to thank God without which none of this would be possible.

Prelude July 21, Present

As I sit down to tell you this story, nearly
ten years after the fact, I have to tell you,
I think sometimes I still don't believe most
of it and I was there for all of it. Well I
was there for most of it. If I didn't have to
see Hank's old face every day, I might think
it were all a bad dream. Jesus it seemed like
two years, but it was just over a month. But,
I'm getting ahead of myself already. Let me
tell you a little about the months leading up
to the day we moved into the building.

I believe it was March of that year and I was
fresh out of the teams on a medical discharge.
My right knee had been taken away by an Iraqi
bullet and been replaced by Dupont plastic and
surgical steel. It happened while saving the
life of a young Marine grunt named Billy
Prescott. He froze because his gun jammed and
I went to pull him out of the line of fire.
Just as I put my leg where his head was I
caught the lead. Way I figure it, better my
knee than his face. Now I didn't know much
about Billy, except he was part of a well to

1

do family from around my neck of the woods, a million miles away back in Oklahoma. Six months later, I was on a plane back to Tulsa for the last time. I was thirty years old, I had my papers, I had my pension and I had a plan. I was gonna open a security firm with a few of my old buddies.

Now it seems that in the time between my knee littering the sand and my plane landing back home, Billy's grandpa, Earnest Prescott passed on. I only found out, because I got a letter saying I was mentioned in the will. Earnest, whom I'd never met, seemed to think I deserved a little something for saving his grandson, young Billy, who, by the way, I hadn't seen since.

This old lawyer handed me the keys and deed to an old research facility that had been sitting empty since the Second World War. He also had it set up so that, after taxes and fees and shit, I was left holding a cool million US. Now don't get me wrong, I have never been happy to hear about someone dying, but his sure made my plan a reality. So I made the calls, bought the equipment and gathered the troops. Four short months later, we had everything and everyone together and were ready to move in.

PART 1 Moving in (Ten Years Earlier)

· July 21

Hank and I drove out to the building in one of our new patrol cars. We had bought a new Plymouth Acclaim and 8 used vehicles from a friendly dealer up in Bristow. We were in the acclaim and the rest of the crew was gonna meet us there later in the day with the vehicles and equipment. We had been by a few days earlier, just drove by, and seeing it now was the same as the first time. When we talked about it later we agreed it looked like time stood still on the other side of the gate.

The layout was pretty simple from where we could see. You had the main building with a big parking lot out front and two cinder block garages off to one side out back. The main building was typical of what you might expect from the 1940's. Big rambling long cinder block and wood, painted white of course. My first thought was that fifty something year old wiring was gonna need a lot of work. It was the first (but far from only) time I was wrong about that building. Public Service said the lights shoulda been turned on yesterday, I had an electrician coming tomorrow and Ma Bell said the phones would be up in a few days. It was gonna take longer for T-1 for the computers, but we could work around that.

Hank unlocked the gate and I drove into the parking lot. I watched him walk up to meet

3

me. Hank at 23 was a big imposing looking
fellow of six foot three and about 310 pounds.
His size and manner mislead most folk into
thinking he was a little slow, but Hank is a
California surfer dude and his regulation
sandy blonde hair is the only betrayal. He is
as nice as they come until its time for
action, then he's one of the few I want havin'
my back. Hank was my second in command as well
as one of the new guard trainers. Everyone in
the patrol division would answer to him. I
trained Hank in teams then pulled some strings
to have him assigned with me later. His time
was up not long after I took the hit for Billy
and he just figured he would roll too. Navy's
loss and I just didn't give a flyin' fuck
cause I was glad to have him with me. Maybe
later he'd wish it was the other way, but it
was done.

 I looked up at the front of my new business,
with its two big windows on the ground floor
and row of twenty across the top. That's when
I noticed the lights on in the center two.

"God I hope that old wiring holds up."

We'd both said it at the same time and it made
my hair stand on end. There was something else
I couldn't quite put my finger on. Hank did.

"Holy shit Chief" His voice was a little
shaky, "did they just repaint this place?"
That's when I noticed it. The paint looked
brand damn new.

"Hell no Hank," I said, listening to the shake
in my own voice, "lawyer said hasn't been
anyone in here since they shut it down during
the war. Hell old Earnest got the place as

part of a settlement, and he never got round to even lookin' at it."

Hank gave me that "don't fuck with me chief" look and said "well then find out what they painted it with, cause I want some of that shit for my place."

Now my curiosity was peeked and we hadn't even opened the door. "Jesus Hank, looks like they just cut the grass and planted fresh flowers." Hank started lookin a little nervous, and I knew he was more than a little superstitious, so I added, "imagine that, someone been jumpin' the fence at night and doing the painting and gardening for us."

Hank smiled and said, "nice of them bastards, huh Chief?"

We walked out back in silence and everything had that same brand damn new look. Hell, even the brass on the one drive through overhead door and the four on the loading dock looked polished. The rear drive, much like the front parking lot, was swept clean.

Hank ambled over to the closer of the two garages and looked through the windows.

"Hey chief," he was actually whispering, "come look, you ain't gonna believe this shit." I hurried to join him at the window. Now of course I noticed the 1940 white Ford ambulance, it was impossible not to, but I also noticed everything else at once. I could see the tools and equipment neatly put away. More than anything else I noticed how everything looked freshly cleaned.

"Why you suppose that's still here?" Hank

asked still whispering.

"Hell if I know, but I bet we can find a use for it."

We didn't really talk about, but we decided we would wait for the others before going inside. My take on it was, safety in numbers, better ten of us get freaked out than just the two of us. I pulled out my cell. I was going to call Ken and find out where they were. Hank took the opportunity to find a shady place to sit. He leaned back against the building and closed his eyes.

"What the fuck!" I yelled, making Hank jump, "less than ten miles from downtown fucking Tulsa and I can't get a damn signal."

Hank just looked at me kinda funny and said "lets walk up by the road and give it another try." It was less than one hundred feet from where we were to the road. It shouldn't have made a difference. We went anyway. I watched the signal meter as we made the short walk. We had no sooner cleared the gate and the meter went to full strength.

"Well don't that just beat the fuck outta anything you ever saw." I walked back inside the gate and it dropped back to nothing. Hank and I each repeated the process several times with the same results. "Fucking Twilight zone,"

Hank half laughed it, "wouldn't surprise me none if ol' Rod whatshisfuck came out saying 'submitted for your approval." It was a bad impression but I laughed my ass off anyway.

"Yeah'" I half joked, "previous tenant,

Stephen King."

I looked back at the building and one of the upstairs lights went off momentarily. I may have imagined it, but I think it winked at me.

I punched Kenny's number, just in time to see the rented U-haul coming down the two-lane, followed by the rest of our crew in the other company vehicles. They were being typical ex-mil shits, had the flashers and sirens going, actin all crazy. Everyone that is, except Bailey and Shannon, our two female partners in crime. They were in the vans and they didn't have any of that shit yet. Ken pulled the U-haul around the back and the rest of em just kinda stopped wherever. Kinda looked like a hostage situation out front just then.

Now would be a good time as any to tell you about my crew.

Hank Miller you already met and he's my number one guy, best friend in the world and closest thing I ever had to a brother.

Then there is Kenneth Fox. Ken and me go way back, our Navy days were before I got in the teams. He was a short wiry dark haired peacock from Wisconsin. He was older than me and had been a Navy Master at Arms on my first ship. Did well for him self, put in his twenty and rolled out with a Chief retirement.

Ken had a head for business and several years as a recruiter made him a pretty good salesman. He would be the sales manager. He would also help train the new guards and salesmen.

Then we have Bailey Kirkwood, 24 years old

with dark brown hair and deep liquid green eyes that could melt a man, like ice cream at a steel beach picnic in the Caribbean. Sweet as honey when she wanted to be and mean as a harpy when you crossed her.

Being Hanks cousin she was another California transplant, with a fresh degree in criminal justice from UCLA. I fell in love the first time I met her and every time I've seen her since. Some things never change.

Bailey was there to take care of the business and legal end of things. She was good at it anyway. Her degree helped her understand the legal mumbo-jumbo.

Our other female is the one and only Shannon (Shay) Steele. Every inch of her six feet and some fraction of an inch is woman. She likes to wear her long sandy blonde hair pulled back in one of those ponytails. God help us all when she lets it down.

Shay would have been great to have on teams, but that wasn't gonna happen was it. She could shoot better than most men I've seen could. She was also the proud holder of two black belts.

I met Shay while I was training her Law Enforcement Class down in Texas. Our friendship helped me get over my first marriage falling apart. We had a brief history and now, although she is five years his senior, Hank is her soul mate.

Shay was the training manager. It was her domain and she carried it well. Her second hat was patrol supervisor. One of those people you were supposed to call when things went wrong.

Next we have Steve (Ice) Poole. We call him that on account of he is always cool; nothing seems to get that man excited, ever! Ice served with me on teams and I always knew I could count on him.

He was a communications expert and I was sure he was gonna have his work cut out for him in the next few weeks.

Coming to us from South Carolina, Ice was about twenty eight that summer but he still had his boyish good looks highlighted by his sandy blonde hair, a little long for my taste, but hey that's life. Only one thing made Ice stand out in a crowd, and that was the scar that ran from his right temple, down to his chin, he got it while helping me pull a young kid out of some bad shit down in Central America.

Ice was the technical manager. He would run the installation department. In addition to being the dispatch supervisor, he helped train the installers and dispatchers.

Shawn Poole is Ice's little brother, now how anyone can call a six foot two hundred pound guy little is beyond me. Shawn and Ice's parents were killed in a smashup in Dorchester County, near Charleston, a few years back and Ice got a hardship.

All they had was each other and that was reason enough for me. Shawn was the assistant installation department manager. He knew the tech stuff almost as good as his brother. They would both help with sales for awhile.

Eddie (Gunner) Winters was a mean son of a bitch retired Gunners Mate chief I met in the

Acey-Ducey club, down at Mayport, when I was a wet behind the ears Second Class. He was only an E-5 back then too but he was still mean.

He was the only man of color in the club and four or five rednecks felt he should leave. Me, I felt otherwise. Now neither of us being very big men, I tried to reason with these Bos' ns, but it just wasn't in their plans to let it go. After Gunner and Me got done with those boys, I can assure you that Chief Boats was gonna have some questions the next mornin' at quarters.

Just a year past forty, Gunner still likes to keep that dome of his shaved clean. Gunner was my armory manager. He knows more about guns than anyone I ever met. He could tell you the location of every gun the company owned. Even when we had over three hundred armed guards.

Now if ever there was a mountain of a man, It had to be Bobby (Bruiser) Parker. Bruiser was born and bred in the hills of West Virginia. Twelve years as a Navy Hull Tech didn't get the backwoods out of that boy. He only stands about five nine, but he's damn near that big around.

A fan of country music and a faithful follower of George Strait and Tracy Lawrence, Bruiser was about as redneck as they come. About most things in life twenty-nine year old Bruiser just "couldn't give a fuck."

Bruiser was the primary night patrol supervisor. He was also the assistant patrol department manager.

Tommy Wantland was the newest member of our rat pack. Kinda a cocky Tom Cruise types, he even got the look down pat, I got to like Tommy when I first met him. (He was writing me a ticket on the Turner for going a bit too fast).

Tommy was an Oklahoma State Trooper, Genuine Smokey the Bear; but, as fate would have it, his ticket almost got punched just a few days past his 23rd birthday, on May 21st. His Caprice decided to shred the left front during a high speed and go end over just a little on the OKC side of the Stroud plaza. You could notice the limp, but only if you knew to look.

I figured he would be good to have around. His short service record showed him to be an outstanding officer. He had connections anyways. Toms' primary mission was to help with training and act as a liaison with local law enforcement agencies.

 Then you are left with me. Brian Kelly, I was thirty that summer and in about the best shape of my life. Only five ten and about one seventy-five I wasn't an overly imposing person physically. I've never been more than average in the looks department. I still had enough military in me to keep the haircut. Back then it was all real dark brown almost black, and still pretty much all there. By the end of August, that would all change.

Most of the crew called me chief then and before long all of them did, including, Ken and Gunner, the other chiefs. Bailey never did. It was always either boss or Bri. My mother used to call me that, damn I hate that name. Course sometimes it's cute when Bailey does it.

Now, we all met in the parking lot that day and everyone kinda looked at the building for a bit before we walked around back to give Ken a hand with the stuff in the truck. As we walked around the back drive Bruiser looks at me and says

"Damn chief this sumbich looks purty good fer an old ass shack."

"Yeah," Ken chimes in, meetin us half way, "thought you said this place had been empty the last fifty or so years."

"It has guy, I swear, but let me show you something you really ain't gonna believe." Hank and I led to the first garage and the old ambulance.

They all stood lookin in the windows like it was some kinda circus sideshow myself included.

Bailey finally said what we all were thinking, "looks like they left for the day and forgot to come back."

It was a simple truth that all of us would come back to several times over the next few days, sometimes we would even repeat it out loud.

    "Well folks," I said after awhile, "let's have a look inside."

"Wait," it was Hank, "ain't we gonna look in the other one?"

He was, of course, talking about the other garage.

I said, "what the hell can't hurt nothin'."

We walked over to garage number two and I

looked through the window on the big wide
door. I got a chill for the second time that
day. The story was much the same as the first
one. It looked like someone had cleaned up for
the day and gone home.

The 1939 Cadillac sedan sitting there shiny
and black held my attention more than any one
thing. Not because it looked new but because
of the dust, or the lack of dust, to be exact.
On the other side of that was a 1937 Chevy
pickup painted in the same white as the
ambulance, on the side were the words
Englewood Foundation, Tulsa-Philadelphia-
Dallas.

 "Well shit" I said, "looks like we got us
some near mint old timey cars boys." "Let's
have a look at the rest."

 It was about noon when I unlocked the back
door into what had been the shipping and
receiving area of the facility, as indicated
by the sign over the door.

Now if you never been to Oklahoma in July let
me tell y'all the temp that day was over 100,
but when I opened that door what came out was
a gust of about 60. Shocked the shit outta
all of us. There were gasps and mumbles from
everyone, including Ice and yours truly.

This part of the facility occupied the entire
back half of the buildings lower floor.

I said "Have a look around in here, lets see
what other cool shit we can find." Nobody
moved for a bit, so I hollered, "shit guys
come on it only an old building, spread out,
damn!" At that point everyone kinda wondered
off in different directions.

I went in search of a light switch, which I
found right by the door we came in.

It was about this time Gunner yelled "hey
boss, come lookit this shit."

Along the front wall starting at the stairs
to the main part of the building and running
the remainder of the room's 300 feet, were
storage cages. About a hundred of them in all
and everyone was damn near full of stuff.
Everything from office supplies to chemicals
and a lot of shit we had no idea of, was in
them cages.

Bailey, who had joined gunner and I about this
time, said, "this stuff must be worth a
fortune."

"Yep" answered Shay, "but what the hell is it
still doing here?" Same question was on my
mind.

"Why the hell not'" I heard Hank yell from
about fifty foot away. "Were in the twilight
zone."

We spent the next hour or so checking out the
stuff in the cages. The amazing part was that
the keys to all but one, were on my ring. The
key to the cage marked A-21 seemed to be
missing; strangest part was the damn thing was
boarded over to top it off.

We messed with the lock, which was different
from the others, for a few minutes. After
awhile I figured it was time to move on and
suggested "we go deeper into the zone."

Now to get from where we were, to where we
wanted to go, one had to climb three steps to
a little four by four landing with a black

pipe hand rail all around. For some reason nine other people felt the need to be on that landing when I opened that door.

Now as luck would have it, or perhaps it was by design, one key on my ring was marked with an "M" and since that was the one that opened the back door, I figured I would try it on this door too. It worked. I guessed it must have been the Master key.

Now again I have to remind you this was a 100 plus degree July day. I remember thinking, if I were a building that had been shut up for such a long time, I am gonna have two things dust and heat and lots of both. When I opened that door however it felt like the same damn near sixty as it was in the bay.

We didn't see much at first on account of the blinds were pulled down over the two big windows, but I found the light switch right by the door where it should be, no surprise there. When I turned it on, now that was a different story altogether.

This room also ran the entire length of the building and was open except for what must have been the supervisor's booth between the two big windows, what definitely were the men's and ladies on the back wall directly opposite the booth and a stairway at each end. The only outside door was right there by the one that we just came through.

The whole room was painted the same white as the outside and the receiving bay. The exception here was the doors were a dark stained wood that stood out in glaring contrast. I remember that now, but none of us noticed any of that because we were looking, staring actually, at the two rows of over one hundred desks in front of us.

Each desk had a typewriter and there was a file cabinet between them. The desks and filers were made of the same dark wood as the doors. That in it's self is not unique what was however, is that every last one of them looked as if someone had been working at them yesterday.

We had entered, what must have been, the typing pool. There were unfinished research notes in more than a few of the typewriters. Sweaters were left hanging on the backs of chairs.

Shay said it for us all that time "hell, looks like they went to lunch and forgot to come back."

"Don't anyone touch a damn thing'" I said. "Not yet anyway, let's just go on upstairs."

The place was giving me the creeps and I wanted to get the rest of the look over with quickly. I was determined we were going to start the business here. The old building was just a little spooky. I had to get used to it first.

We met at the top of the stairs here things were different. The hall had hard wood floors, instead of what must have been asbestos tile downstairs and the walls were richly paneled. There were twenty offices on one side and eighteen on the other. Fortunately for us the keys to these were numbered.

I gave everyone a couple of keys each and kept

the ones to the two back center offices, and
what appeared to be one big one in the front.
I wanted to turn those lights off.

 In spite of my best efforts everyone stayed
together and I opened most of the doors with
my master key. The four offices at the top of
the stairs were the first ones we opened. We
got such a creepy feeling when we opened them.
We closed and locked the doors quickly without
giving them much of a look.

When it came time to open the big office
everyone was together. I think we half
expected to see a fat man sitting there
smoking a fat cigar. Maybe that would have
been better.

What we did see when we opened the door was a
huge cherry wood desk with ivory inlays and a
glass top. In fact, the shelves and file
cabinets were all made of the same material.
Behind that desk was the most beautiful chair
I had ever seen. It was rich leather, tanned
in the same deep cherry as the desk.

I made the decision then that this would be my
office. I didn't see the need to change a
thing. Except for the telephone. That big
black ugly phone would have to go.

"Hell," I half said half thought, "first damn
phone I've seen in here." And it was.

Have you ever walked into a new house,
apartment, or office for the first time and
saw a phone? For some unexplainable reason you
pick it up, even though you know it ain't
hooked up yet. Well I was no exception. I
picked up this fifty-year-old phone, put it to
my ear and heard the damnedest thing. A dial

tone.

"It fuckin works, the damn thing works."

I must have been a little on the pale side, cause all these people are looking at me. I felt like I was a sideshow freak.

Just as I put the receiver back on the cradle my cell rang. I didn't answer it. I couldn't bring myself to. I shut off the lights, locked the door and walked away with the damn thing ringing.

We went back out the way we came in locking things up behind us.

I said to Ken, "Hey just park the truck in the Bay and we'll get it tomorrow."

His reply surprised me. "Sure chief, hey Ice want to ride with me."

He looked scared, a little anyway. I couldn't blame him. Ice and I both rode with him, what the hell, we were all a little spooked that day.

After we collected the vehicle keys I told everyone I'd "see them at nine." Hank took everyone back to their POV's in one of the vans. All except Bailey and me, we took the acclaim.

I glanced up as I locked the gate and said "FUCK," the light was back on.

"Bri'" she says to me as we head down SH 69, "we are all adults and most of you guys have seen more shit than most normal people can handle." "So what the hell were we so afraid of?"

"Just a lot of shit we weren't expecting

babe," was all I could give her.

July 22

I pulled up to the gate about 8:45 to find Hank, Shay and Gunner waiting for me.

"Suck-ups" I hollered jokingly as I unlocked the gate.

"Suck this," was the reply and I still don't know who from.

We were just getting parked when Ice and Shawn pulled in, the tires on Ice's lovingly restored 69 Hemi Cuda, complaining from the abuse. Bailey's Mustang not far behind. By the time I got to the door everyone was there but Tom. I knew he was seeing the doc, so we were all there for now.

Everything looked exactly like we left it last night. However, it felt different, more peaceful, at rest. Just to make sure I went and looked. The light in my office was off.

We spent the better part of that morning unpacking the U-haul and the rest of the vehicles, which had by now been moved to the back. About the time Tom showed up from his weekly with the torture therapist.

I sent Hank and Shay down to McDonalds to get us all some lunch. We were all feeling pretty good about then, sitting in the typing pool (which would later be known as simply "the pool") the jitters of yesterday all but forgotten and that's when it happened.

Simple thing really, just a fifty-year-old phone ringing upstairs. Don't ask me why I looked at my watch just then, but I did. It was 12:21. Didn't any of us answer it. When it finally stopped ringing I handed Bailey my cell.

"Give Ma bell a yell see what the hell is up with that phone."

"Get right on it Boss," she sassed, but she was smiling.

She wasn't smiling when she got off the phone. The rest of us weren't smiling for long.

"Lady said they will have our lines run sometime today. They will be here tomorrow sometime to start the inside work." She hesitated and looked at me kinda sideways. "Bri, she also said that there hasn't been a line to this building for at least thirty years. Not since they went to burying them. Hell there hasn't even been a poll for one since then."

It was about then Hank and Shay got back with the Big Mac's and such. Before long we were all back to the norm.

I figured out that since the Phone guys would be there, we had better figure out where we wanted them. Of course the Supervisors booth was the perfect place for the dispatcher and I *knew* where my office was. The rest was a guess.

I told everyone to find an office upstairs and settle in. I figured we would set up a few of extra offices. We would need two for the admin staff and several for sales.

Turns out everyone took an office real close to mine. We were all kinda huddled up like.

Bailey and Hank took the two directly across from mine. Not Shawn though. He decided to take one all the way down at the far end.

"It gives me a little breathin room."

I didn't have a problem with it at the time. Thinking about it now, I don't think it made a difference.

We figured we would leave the downstairs pretty much as it was. We would need to add a break room and bunkroom. Of course we would have to add an extra door at the other end in case of a fire.

About four thirty we had all the computers set up and were finishing up the dispatcher stuff. There was a knock on the door. I walked to the door thinking, *"who the hell knocks at a business."* I was greeted at the door by a PO-dunk from PSO. What he had to say damn near literally knocked me to the floor.

"Hey buddy," he said with a grin I will never forget, "just wanted to let you know I got your power on."

When I could speak I said "Powers been on since yesterday."

He looked at me like I was from Mars and said, "Nawsir I just put the connecting fuses on the poll."

I thanked him and closed the door. Tom Looks up from the terminal in the booth and smiles "whatcha make a that shit boss?"

"Well, I say it's about time we call it a day." "What y'all think?" I don't remember hearing any arguments.

 I rode home with Bailey that day. We just didn't feel like being alone. Neither of us talked much the rest of that night. Figure we'd had enough for one day. We just needed to enjoy the nearness of each other.

Keep in mind, we was just getting close back then. I fell asleep on her living room sofa, holding her. wondering what exactly *"I did make of that shit."*

July 23

 I woke that morning feeling hung over. I
didn't even get the pleasure of the previous
nights drunk. Took me a bit to realize where I
was.

Sometime during the night sweet Bailey had
taken my shoes off and covered me up. Of
course I don't remember being cold but a woman
will do things like that anyway.

She hadn't gone far. She was curled up, on her
love seat, with a blanket of her own. She
wasn't asleep. I know this cause her green
eyes were looking at me across the coffee
table. I winked and she blessed me with a
sleepy smile.

"Guess we better get around. I need to run you
by your place, so you can get a shower and
change." This time she winked," don't want
those fools getting the wrong idea about us
now do we?"

 She dropped me at the house. She was probably
ordering breakfast for us, at the Village Inn,
by the time I backed my Ram Charger out to go
meet her, Hank and Shay.

None of us mentioned the phone or the electric issues of the previous day at breakfast. None of us said much of anything to be exact. We exchanged social comments, ate our breakfast and drove to work all in a line, like a funeral.

When we got there, the side of the road was lined with cars. It was this that led me to decide, until we got up and running, I'd make everyone a copy of the gate key. Wouldn't need it after that.

Three of Ma Bells gray and white vans were waiting to install our inside lines. My spark-trician was there too. I told him to start with the boxes and check the wiring.

"Let me know how bad the damages are."

Bailey went with the phone guys to get them started. I went off with Ken and Hank to talk about hiring the rest of the staff. We needed more guards and dispatchers. We would have to handle the sales and installs, until we got help. We already had several clients waiting.

Things went pretty well for a while, most everyone was upstairs getting their offices personalized and shit, Hank Ken and I were huddled around a couple of desks in the pool when the electrician gives me the first of three surprises that day.

"Mr. Kelly," he said, "you really should replace the fuses with breakers and them old two prongs with threes not to mention some GFCI's in the facilities but the old wires look brand new."

Only thing I could say was "do what needs to

be done."

 The second surprise came at 12:21; I checked
my watch again not for the last time, when the
phone rang. Scared the living shit out of the
phone guy, who just happened to be setting up
the rig in my office at the time. He answered
it, but there was no one on the other end, *go
figure guess they hung up.*

 The third surprise came a little later. Poor
Hank went to take advantage of the privacy
offered by one of the two gents' rooms
upstairs. Seems that somehow the door got
locked from the outside. No matter how hard he
tried, he couldn't get it opened. He removed
it instead. It cost me three hundred for a new
one. If you had seen the look on his face
you'd agree. It was worth every dime.

 We waited for the service guys to finish up.
The phone guys were done. Sparkey told me he
had one more fuse box to replace but he
wouldn't be back for a few days. After they
left, we all went home.

I had dinner with Bailey and the Poole
brothers. Afterwards, Her and I went to my
place. We had a couple of drinks and watched
the news. Then we settled in for another night
on the sofa.

July 25

 I got to the office late on account of a
meeting with the city. By the time I arrived,
everyone else had been there awhile. Bailey
and Ice were in the pool going over a stack of
phone messages and setting appointments.

"Seems our ads paid off chief," Ice informs me
of the obvious.

Bailey adds "On both ends, we got twenty
applicants and twice that many leads."

"Well Hell," I said, with no mock surprise,
"Ice you, Shay, Shawn and Tom take the leads.
Hank, Eddie, Bruiser and I will handle the
interviews. Bailey, why don't you see if you
can get Ken to get our system installed
today."

"Already on that one boss," I hear Ken call
form somewhere. Quieter he adds "Damn acting
like a manager already, been in business a
week and don't know what the hells goin' on."

"Bailey," I ask acting like I didn't hear Ken,
"when is the first interview?"

"Eleven, in your office."

 The rest of the morning was pretty busy,
doing the mundane shit, holding interviews,

and making sales calls. Everyone was near my office around 12:20 and sure enough the phone rang right on time.

This time I answered it. What I heard made my blood run cold, a male voice that sounded a million miles away.

"Keep a close eye on that A-21 experiment Jacob" and then, the line went dead.

"Boys before we go home today I want that fucking A-21 cage opened"

What I felt must have showed on my face, because they all just nodded and went back to their lunch. I couldn't eat, not for awhile anyway. Right then I wanted to cut that phone line, I didn't think it would do any good. I still don't know why.

The rest of the afternoon was very busy, between the four of us we agreed on about six patrol guys and two dispatchers.

I had all but forgotten about my phone call until about 4:30. I look up and see Bruiser holding the bolt cutters. He and Hank both got shit eatin grins on their faces.

Bruiser says, "come on Chief lets go find out what's in that fuckin cage."

We were joined, on the way down, by the entire staff. It seemed everyone wanted to see what A-21 was all about.

I got to the cage and looked at my friends.

"Ok you guys stand back I don't know what the hell's in there."

"Fuck Dat," was Gunner's reply "we're in this shit together Chief."

That seemed to be the general feeling among the troops.

"Ok," I resigned, "but Shay you and Bailey please step back a bit. Now! Please!" I cut off any objection before it started. "Bruiser, will you cut the damn thing already?"

When Bruiser cut the lock the door swung open. Nervously we entered A-21.

I still don't know to this day what exactly had been in A-21. From what I could tell, what ever it was had been at least partially made of iron. It looked as if it had melted at some point in time, iron and all, and was just a big lump on the floor.

Before I could ask, Tom gave me the answer.

"I got a friend at the OSBI crime lab that will come down and have a look." "On the hush of course."

"Of course," I said "see what you can do."

With that, we were done for the day. I went home not sleeping very well.

July 26

The morning started out pretty rough. I get all kinds of hell first thing when I get through the door.

First, I got Ice hollering, "every fuckin thing's been moved around in dispatch."

As it turns out, this was true with just about every other office we had touched. Small things missing too. Nothing major was missing. Mostly personal things were just fucking gone. Ken needed to get our system finished today. No signs of forced entry but I wasn't going to take any chances.

The rest of the morning was pretty quiet; we did a few interviews. The sales guys were busy calling on our new clients. Lots of new construction up in Owasso. Big expensive homes, with expensive shit, the kinda shit that needed safeguarding. Looked like things were going good for us.

When the phone rang at 12:21 I picked it up without thinking. We were all pretty busy at that point. Thankfully Jacob had no mystery caller that day, just a little static and then the dial tone that shouldn't have been there.

Just for the hell of I picked the phone back up and dialed my office private line. What the caller ID showed me made no sense. In fact it was impossible.

The name said Englewood but the number said 555-821-1942. In case you are wondering the AC for Tulsa is 918 and if you ask around there is no 555 AC. At least not one I am aware of anyway.

For laughs I díaled the number leaving out the Area Code and got a supermarket. Then I tried it with a 555. I got Ma Bell's recorded were sorry shit. I gave up on it.

About two, the sign guy showed up with our new Kelly security signs.

"Finally gonna look like pro's" Bailey informed me.

He took the Englewood signs down from the Roof and over the gate and put ours in their place.

We locked the old signs in Garage one with the Ambulance. Just in case someone ever came asking about them. I didn't figure anyone would, but you never knew.

I asked Bailey to do me some research on Englewood Foundation and see what she could come up with.

"I ain't in no hurry and I really don't expect much, but give it a shot Just the same."

"Sure Boss and by the way Tom and his guy from the state are out in the bay, looking over that lump in A-21." "Shit why didn't some one tell me."

I hauled my ass out to the bay. I needed to know what was up.

Tom's guy was taking samples from the lump in the cage. He kept saying shit like "I ain't never" and "what the hell is this stuff."

Finally he looks at me and says, "Mr. Kelly, I know we were gonna do this on the hush, but I think I better get EPA out here pretty quick. Hell I don't even know what some of this shit is."

My reply was "well Tom show the man to the phone." My thoughts, on the other hand, were "*great EP fuckin A, I got to pay to clean up someone else's mess.*"

It was about then that the guys started coming in from the field. Ken was happy to informed me that "our system is up and running."

"Just need to run a few tests real quick."

Then to really make my day Shay says, "Love the new signs boss, but you really should think about putting those Englewood signs out back or something."

"What the hell are you talking about Shay." I think I shouted, "those signs are in the garage with the…"

The look on her face told me they weren't anymore. "I'm the only one with a key and…I. Well shit."

We all went out front to have a look. Sure enough there they were side by side leaning against the front of the building, looking freshly painted to boot. Big Wrought Iron things they were. Had a big ugly crow looking piece of shit right on of top the arc.

"Boys give me a hand with these. Ken, get those tests done and arm the fuckin garages first. After that, lets get the hell outta here."

 I was really happy to call it a day. The shit was getting weirder by the minute.

I went home alone and had Subway in front of the Channel 6 at 6:00. I dozed just in time to miss seeing my first real TV commercial. I dreamed about Crows carrying signs and making phone calls at 12:21 to a phone that didn't exist.

July 27

 I decided to get an early start on things, so
I skipped the normal breakfast meeting and
headed straight to the office. The light
burning in my office or how the place still
looked freshly mowed no longer surprised me.
"*I wonder how it looks in winter.*"

I'm not sure how surprised I was to see them
damn wrought iron Englewood Foundation signs,
leaning against the front of the building,
like we'd never moved them.

"Gonna take care of that for sure today."

I knew there wasn't anyone around to hear it,
but I said it out-fuckin-loud anyway.

 As I unlocked the door and punched in the
alarm code a funny thought occurred to me.
Here we have the state of the art in security
systems and the only damn place it's monitored
is inside the building it was installed to
protect. "*Is that fuckin ironic or what, Good
Morning Mr. Serling*"

 I came to realize quickly, that I had never
been in the building alone before. It gave me
an uneasy feeling as I made my way to the

booth, to check last nights activity report, for our one active system.

The fact that everything was rearranged was not lost on me, I simply chose to ignore it.

Now, because our computers monitor the system, any activity will send a note to the dispatcher's terminal. In a perfect world, the dispatcher would then notify the facility contact person, the zone patrol unit and the appropriate authorities.

However, in this case, there was no dispatcher, so no one could call the Facility Contact, me in this case, or notify the zone patrol unit, wouldn't be in place for a few days yet anyway or call the police. Any alarm signals would, however, be sent to the terminal and should still be on the screen.

It was and by sheer dumb ass luck the printer was set to auto logging. What this meant was what ever went to the screen would also printed on the Dot Matrix printer.

I tore the printout off not really believing what I saw.

Activity Date 07/26/92 Tuesday:

   1730 Kelly Security Act code 00001 System active unoccupied mode.

Activity Date 07/27/92 Wednesday:

   0021 Kelly Security Act code 00001 Intrusion Door alarm (silent) activated Zone 1 point 1 "Building 1 Main Entrance door" Delay timeout.

   0023 Kelly Security Act code 00001 Intrusion Door alarm (silent) activated Zone 3 point 2

"Building 2 Overhead Door" No delay.

0030 Kelly Security Act code 00001 Intrusion
Door alarm reset Zone 3 point 2 "Building 2
Overhead Door"

0033 Kelly Security Act code 00001 Intrusion
Door alarm reset Zone 1 point 1 "Building 1
Main Entrance"

0815 Kelly Security Act code 00001 System Mode
Change Zone 1 occupied Zone 2 occupied Zone 3
Active Zone 4 Active Access point 1 "Building 1
Main Entrance" Operator 101 "Brian Kelly"

I decided to leave the dispatchers office the
way it was, even though I knew Ice was gonna
be pissed again. We had a busy day ahead. The
guys would be coming today to put in the false
walls for the bunk and Break rooms. We still
had more people to hire and my makeshift sales
force had more work than they could handle.
Ken and Ice were starting installs. I didn't
have the slightest intention on, spending the
best part of the morning, putting things back
the way they were.

Sitting in the pool, I made a few decisions.
We would keep about 10 desks in the pool area
for the bullpen. We might as well keep the
typewriters and file cabinets for report
writing. We would sell the rest along with
most of the stuff in the receiving area. We
sure as hell didn't need it. I was sure
someone could put it to good use.

I made notes to have Bailey look into
getting the legal stuff together on the old

cars out back, as well as, keep looking into Englewood Foundation. I also was going to need to have Ice rig the system to call my cell when our alarm was set off.

I still had a little time before everyone started showing up. I took this time to do some snooping. I checked several of the desks and files. All I found was a lot of research information. I couldn't find one single piece of personal information. That got me curious. By the time the crew started showing up, I had abandoned the pool and moved to the upstairs offices.

With the exception of our stuff, I couldn't find one piece of personal data. Hell, I couldn't even find files on employees. I reluctantly gave up my search, when I heard Bailey down in the pool.

Bailey was making coffee and talking to Shay and Hank. I showed the printout to Hank and asked, "what you make of that?"

He just stood there studying it. I decided to let him think on it a bit. I gave my notes to Bailey and told her to see what she could get done.

"The priority there is the cars and selling this junk ok."

"Sure Bri, missed you at the Village this morning."

She smiled and I could tell she was glad her admin people were starting today. They were temps, but they would do for now. It would take some of the load off her and help us get the staff straight.

Bailey went back to the coffee and I looked to Hank.

"Now chief, looks to me like someone came in here for some reason, then went out to the garage and moved those signs."

"Not exactly Hank," I replied "looks more like someone left here, went out and moved those signs, then came back."

He gave me a puzzled look and said, "only problem with that theory chief, is those motion detectors up there are hooked to the alarms and they make a hell of a noise."

"That my friend," I said with a smile, "is the whole fucking problem. It don't matter which fuckin theory you subscribe to."

Tom was at his weekly doc's appointment; last one he would got to for awhile. Gunner and Bruiser were off to OK City in the on of the vans, to pick up our portable communications gear, so I knew they were gonna be late.

Ken, Ice and Shawn took the two half tons and went straight to their first installs. That left Shay to handle sales calls. Hank and me were the only ones around to do the rest of the interviews.

By the end of the day we would have hire all we were going to for awhile. However, there was nothing going on now. That being the case, I put them to work looking for any personal or personnel information and any information on A-21.

Around ten, applicants started showing up. We abandoned our search once again. Hank and I started doing interviews and Shay settled in her office making and returning sales calls.

Bailey had commandeered a couple of the overflow offices for her admin temps and had them squared away. From the sound of things, she had them working on something already. She was in her office working, away at her Packard Bell. It was business as usual until, well, 12:21 and you know what happened then. I didn't answer.

Shortly after the call, Tom showed with his guy from the crime lab and a couple of scary looking thugs from the EPA. By the time I got to the Bay the EPA goons were on their cells. Tom came over to meet me.

"Boss, these guys don't know what that shit is either. Funny thing, they had a look around and got on the phone with the Department of Defense. They got a fellow on his way here now from the Tulsa DIS and another two or three coming by chopper from Tinker and Ft. Sill."

"Holy fuck, like I need this shit," I swore.

"Hell boss, they been looking at some of this shit in the other cages and talking on their cells ever since. Guess we got some nasty shit on our hands here."

The last part he didn't need to add.

Those EPA goons never said a word to me. They just waited until the DIS got there and left without saying goodbye. Not that I missed talking to them mind you.

Now this DIS fellow was a different story. He walked right up to me and stuck out his hand.

"Chief Kelly," at least he was trying to get

on my good side, "I'm Special Agent in Charge Mike Evans." I just nodded. "The only thing I can tell you is, some of the stuff you have here is Mil Spec. Now if you don't mind we are gonna take it off your hands."

I stood my ground and gave him a defiant look. I wasn't going to be pushed around. He needed to know that.

"Fine by me Agent Evans, But, you are gonna catalog every thing you take out of here. My man Tom here's gonna be with you the whole time. Got a problem with that, Agent Evans, and you can get A Fucking Warrant." He didn't have a problem.

The Military guys game and took a bunch of shit out in trucks. Tom got a copy of the list and Agent Evans assured him we would be compensated for our troubles.

Gunner and Bruiser got back and I had them haul those old signs down to the scrap yard. Nothing like overkill to take care of a problem that never should have existed.

Ken, Ice and Shawn got in about five. I remembered to have Ice set the system up to call my cell.

He kinda laughed when he said, "from the looks of that report, I'd say don't go to bed until around one."

I shot him the bird and left him with it.

We all left the office around six and went to have dinner at Don Pablo's. We had a pretty good time. Even Shawn joined in, which made Ice feel good.

My cell did ring at 12:21 am but it wasn't
the system calling me it was 555-821-1942. Of
course when I answered there was no one there.

July 28

My house phone pulled me out of a deep sleep;
I checked the alarm clock I'd for got to set.
It smiled back at me 9:45.

"Yeah," was about all I could manage. It was
Bailey

"Boss, sorry to wake you, but you might want
to get your ass down here, we got some
problems."

I could hear Ice and Hank yelling and cussing
in the background.

" Fifteen Minutes," I told her and hurried to
get dressed.

It was more like twenty by the time I got my
shit together and got there. The whole crew,
as well as, a group of the new recruits met
me. Hank got to me first.

"Now Chief the log was clear, just when you
set the system and when Bailey opened up this
morning."

"Well, so, what's the problem then Hank?"
I was annoyed but it wasn't his fault.

"Someone's been in the Bay, nothings where it

should be."

"Let's go," I told him and he led the way.

The bay looked like a battle zone. Shit was everywhere. That's how it looked at first. Fact was, everything we had stored in one of the cages had been taken out and stacked neatly in the bay. It only looked scattered, because it wasn't where it should have been there.

Anything missing?" I asked anyone that heard.

Ken answered me, partly because internal security was his thing.

"So far nothing is gone, well nothing's missing anyway."

"Ok full inventory, Ken, you and Shay handle that. The rest of you have new hires to train. Let's get to work. Ken, we will help you get that put away later."

"Sure thing boss, sure thing."

Back in the pool, Bailey gave me some more good news.

"Bri, we got two accounts set to go online tonight and we won't have a night crew until Monday."

"Well don't that just shave the Pu… er cat."

I was glad I caught myself. There just some words you don't use around Bailey and I had almost learned one of them the hard way, again.

"Get the Staff together after lunch and we will figure something out."

"Already set the meeting for one, everyone

will be here boss."

"Well hell," I said mostly under my breath, "Glad I wasn't the last to know. At least those fucking signs weren't out front."

She gave me the smile, that "f" word not withstanding.

"Be thankful for something. And also no luck on the search for the Englewood Foundation anywhere."

"Didn't figure on it," I shook my head.

"Well," she hesitated "there is one more thing."

Her not coming straight out with it told me this one was the big one. I just waited.

"We checked the VIN's with DMV and they have no record of them being registered, anywhere, to anyone, ever. It's not much of a problem though. Because they were part of the property, they belong to you. Just take a few days to get through the red tape."

Still didn't make any sense, but again, what did around here.

"Ok, I'll be in my office"

I got so involved in invoices and other paper work; it surprised me when Shay tapped on my open door.

"Chief you coming to the meeting?"

I checked my watch 1:10.

"Sure coming, hey Shay"

"Yeah Chief," She looked puzzled.

"First time since we moved in, no phone

call."

She looked at the phone and shrugged. We went downstairs.

The other eight senior staff members were huddled around four of the ten remaining desks in the pool, drinking coffee. Shay and I pulled up chairs and made it complete.

We all knew why we were there, so I got right down to it.

"Ok who wants to camp out with me tonight? Tom, you, Ken and Gunner got families so you're off the hook, no questions. Hank, you and me are stuck here no matter what. I need volunteers to help cover tonight, tomorrow and the weekend."

Shay, as expected, was the first to chime in.

"I'm with Hank so count me in."

Ice and Shawn raised their hands too. Before Bruiser could pony up, I let him off the hook.

"Bruiser I need you fresh tomorrow to train the troops, so maybe the weekend ok."

"Sure chief," he looked disappointed. "Kinda like to be here the first night is all."

"Well Bruiser. I ain't gonna make you go home."

He brightened at this. "Ok then I'm staying."

"So then Ice get those systems up and let's get down to business. Any of the rest of you need to go get a few things make it quick." I added one final thing. "Bailey have your temps put together a makeshift schedule"

"Sure Bri we'll get it done right away. Why

don't you give me your keys? I'll run by your place with Shay and pick your stuff up."

"Thanks," I said tossing her my keys, "you're the best."

"Don't ever forget it."

This was followed by her heartbreaking smile. As I went back to my office I heard Tom.

"Hey Bailey, tell your girls to find a way to work Ken, Gunner and me into the weekend day shift."

"Man I love my crew."

The rest of the day went by quick. By the time it was over we had a team of six dispatchers and eighteen security guards, on rotating shifts, starting Monday.

Bailey's schedule had it set up so Shay, Hank, Ice and me would rotate through dispatch, starting with me. When we weren't in the booth, we were in the ready or bunkroom, waiting to respond as necessary.

Our two active clients expected monitoring and response this weekend. They knew they wouldn't have regular patrols until Monday. *"Thank God for small favors."*

About six, just as things started getting quiet, Bailey shows up looking showered and fresh with a bucket of KFC, complete with fixins, and her overnight bag.

"What?" She smiled noticing my look. "Hey I'm not gonna let you guys have all the fun." To me she whispered "safety in numbers, right boss?"

"Let's hope" was all I had to offer.

About nine, things had calmed down to
nothing. Ice and Shawn were snoring away
already in the bunkroom. Hank, Shay and
Bruiser had been watching an old movie, on a
19-inch that had, some how, made its way into
the pool.

Bruiser was already gone and from the looks
of him Hank wasn't far behind. Shay with that
long ass hair down was leaned back against
Hank, oblivious to everything.

As for Bailey and I, we were in the booth
talking about all that stuff two people,
getting close, talk about. You know the stuff,
the past, the future, kids, that kind of
thing.

Looking at her then in her cotton button up,
blue jeans and Nike's, with her hair just
washed and brushed, just barely dry and no
make-up, not that she ever wore much.

I figured she was about the most wonderful
creature the Almighty ever created. From where
I was sitting, it appeared he'd spent a little
extra time on that one.

Just listening to her talk would have been
enough to make Elton put away his funny hats
and glasses and lock the closet forever. She
sounded even better than she looked, if that
was possible. Her voice was silky smooth and
soft as a light rain on a spring night.

Of all the things that happened that night,
only one was good. That night removed any
doubt, from either of our minds, which way our
relationship was going. I fell hard in love
with the woman that was Bailey Kirkwood! It
was a little different for her. She just kinda

slipped into it gently, like a cat slinking down the stairs. It only took her a little longer. Either way the result was the same. Which was just fine by me.

Hank relieved me in the booth about quarter till twelve.

"Chief" he said to me, "this place feels better at night than in the day."

"Sure is peaceful." I replied, knocking gently on the wooden booth door.

Shay and Bailey were in a corner of the pool talking girl talk I guessed. I tossed them a good night wave and fell into the bunkroom to get a little shut eye. I just didn't know how little.

July 29

Next thing I knew, I got Bailey shaking me
awake. Meanwhile, Shay is working to get the
Poole brothers out of the rack. Both of them
girls looked like the ghost of Mr. Chicken-
shit walked up and kissed them.

"Brian."

Bailey's tone was a calm that didn't come
anywhere close to matching her look, not to
mention she called me Brian, just used the
whole name. Didn't even do that the first time
we met, it was always Bri.

"There is a gawd awful noise coming out of
the bay." She took a Deep Breath. "Hank and
Bruiser were gonna check it out, but the
fucking lights won't come on."

There, she had said the "F" word. Now I was
sure something was wrong. Not that I needed
to, but one glance at my Timex told me it was
12:21.

I could hear the racket, from the bay, in the
bunkroom. I grabbed my shoes and headed out to
the pool. Hank and Bruiser were huddled in the
open door to the bay. Made me think of a

couple of teen age boys looking through the whorehouse window.

I had to laugh at the thought, in spite of myself. If the others noticed, they didn't comment, but they must have thought I'd totally lost it.

Hank grabbed my arm and says, "Chief, something's raising holy hell out there and *that's* where all our gear is."

He had a good point. He also had the shotgun we kept in the booth.

"Ice," I whispered over my shoulder, "run and get my gear bag from the back seat of my car and my nine from the glove box."

I tossed him my keys and he hit the ground running. We all held our breath, because, even over the ruckus in the bay, we could all hear the only phone in the place that still had a bell.

I kept the ready bag in my car as a hold over from my days on the teams. In it, among other things, was two six "D" cell Mag-lights. I handed One light to Bruiser and the other to Ice.

"Bruiser, you're with me. Hank, you and Ice count to five and follow. Keep those lights and that gut buster pointed towards the far end of the bay. Let's move."

As soon as Bruiser and I hit the first step into the bay the noise stopped. He hadn't even turned on the flashlight and didn't need to, because about then all the lights in the place came on.

On instinct, my eyes went to the breaker box on the back wall by the door. Closed, even still had the car seal through the loops.

Bruiser, feeling the need to speak, said, "sure is fucking cold in here."

He was right, cold enough to see your breath. Hank and Ice revised my plan and came up beside us. Ice had the Mag-light in his hand it was still on, but unnecessary.

I took a closer look at the other end of the bay. The door to every cage stood open. Even the ones Ken had put new locks on earlier. The lone exception was A-21. "*Well why the fuck ain't I surprised.*

I walked to the nearest cage and slammed the door hard. It was loud enough, but the sound was wrong. Even if all of them were slamming at the same, time it still wouldn't explain what we heard.

Next, I walked back to the gun safe, which served as our armory, next to the door. At least it was still locked. I fixed that quick and gave everyone a nine. I took a couple of extras to Bailey, Shay and Shawn, who were waiting at the still open door. I gave one of the nines and the shotgun to Shay.

"You and Bailey go watch the booth." The other nine I gave to Shawn. "Come on, help us look for the source of that damn noise."

It wasn't exactly by design, but we spread out across the bay like a bunch of Airdales doing a FOD walkdown. We were close enough to see each other, but we could cover the whole area. Ironically, it was Shawn that found what we were looking for.

"Hey Chief," it was the first time he'd called me that, "Come over here quick! You gotta fuckin see this shit!"

"Whatcha got Shawn?"

I yelled on the run, nine at the ready. The kid was pointing at the floor. At something I'd never noticed.

There in the floor, smack dab in the middle of the bay, in a spot everyone of us had walked on a hundred times, was a four by four metal plate.

"How the hell did we miss this?" I really didn't want an answer.

The plate was split in the middle, with a handle on each piece; the kinds that slide in when closed, with hinges on each side. It was a big door that went right into the bay floor. I picked up one side of the door and dropped it. That, was damn sure the noise we heard.

"Hank, you and Bruiser go grab me a length of gate chain and a lock. Ice, you and Shawn stay with me."

Bruiser and Hank brought me the chain and lock. I wrapped it several times around the handles, made sure it was tight and locked it.

"Let's get back inside," I told them. "Grab some more lights out of that cage. Might as well hang on to them guns, just in case."

As we walked back to the pool, Shawn grabbed my arm.

"Chief, I swear, The only reason I noticed that thing was because of the light around the edges."

I turned the lights off in the bay and looked towards the hole. I couldn't see any light. It was enough to make my flesh crawl and my exhaust port pucker. I tried not to show it.

"We'll check it in the morning."

Now, if we had been in combat, or chasing some bad guy, nothing in the world would have stopped any one of us from checking that hole then and there. But this wasn't combat and we all knew it. Some how, at that point, we knew we weren't up against some bad guy.

What I was feeling must have shown on my face when I walked back into the pool, cause Bailey came to me and put her arms tight around me. I was happy for it. Glad for the closeness, glad for her touch. We walked together to the break room and relaxed on the couch. The others joined us soon enough. Not wanting to talk, but not wanting to be alone. *"Safety in numbers."*

I don't know when it happened, but at some point, I must have drifted to sleep. Right there in the safety of Bailey's arms.

Funny how full-grown, well-trained, combat vets can feel safe in the arms of a scant hundred pounds of femininity. Ain't love some shit.

She woke me, about ten, with a gentle touch and a cup of coffee. I didn't intend to do it. I kissed her without thinking. Just a soft, quick brush, on the lips, but a kiss none the less. She didn't hesitate; she leaned forward and kissed me back. Not a brush this time and not quick but just as soft and gentle. Yep, I was falling for sure and it seemed she was hitchin a ride.

Out in the pool, business was happening. Patrolmen and dispatchers were being trained. Everyone was doing his or her job, business as usual.

Myself, well I had nothing to do and really had no desire to face my office, so I just hung around the pool most of the day.

During the lunch break, I was about ready to have a look in the hole. Only thing stopping me was the ringing from my office, I figured I would at least wait until it stopped.

A young kid, dispatcher to be, asked "isn't someone gonna answer that?"

"Nah," was Ken's reply from the booth. "They want Jacob and he ain't here right now."

"Hey Ken," I say, "Round up Ice, Tom, Hank, Gunner and Bruiser and meet me in the bay. I think we need to have a look in that hole."

A few minuets later, I was in the bay surrounded by my entire senior staff. Save for Bailey, who was upstairs with her admin team, working on duty rosters and CLEET certifications.

I had to ask, "who's minding the children?"

Ken had the answer. "Well, that one experienced dispatcher we hired seems to know her shit and she's in the booth. Figure she can yell at me if she has any problems."

It wasn't until then I noticed that, in addition to side arms and flashlights, everyone had radios on their duty belts. Except for me. *"Out of the fucking loop again hey Bri."*

"Oh well lets do this."

I unlocked the pad lock and we pulled open both the steel plates.

We looked down into the hole at a set of wooden stairs that went down about eight feet, ending at a dirt floor. There was a concrete wall behind the stairs. By shining my light, I could see a hallway running the other way about 150 feet, lined with catacombs on each side. From where I was that was all I could see.

"Ok, Hank, Ice and Bruiser, you are with me, the rest of you wait up here and make damn sure those doors don't close."

No arguments this time, it was clear to everyone who was in charge.

We all switched on our Mags and the four of us headed into the hole. Me in the lead, followed by Hank, then Bruiser, with Ice bringing up the rear.

About half way down the steps, I saw the light switch. Remembering what Shawn had told me, I figured I'd give it a try. Six lights came on at once in the hall, as well as one light in each of the catacombs.

They weren't just catacombs. They were cages. Not like the ones up in the bay that held supplies. These looked more like the kind of cages that held people. From the looks of the bars, they had not been very nice ones.

Each Cell was about fifteen by fifteen, with a bunk and light in each. There were nineteen in all, running both sides of the hall. The First one on the right had a desk and file cabinet, like the ones in the pool and no bars.

All the cells were unlocked and we checked each one. The last one held all the stuff that had come up missing over the last few days.

Hank and Bruiser gathered the missing items, while Ice and I checked that file cabinet. There were plenty of files with no names, just numbers and a whole lot of "behavior notes."

We grabbed as many of those files at a time as we could and passed them up until the cabinet was empty. I figured; we would find as many answers here, as we were likely to get.

That done, I followed the guys up the stairs turning out the light as I went. Once back in the bay, I re-locked the doors.

"Lets get these files inside. I have a feeling we are all gonna be doing some reading soon."

We took the files to the pool and filled up one of the empty cabinets.

"Push this thing over by the booth and chain it shut. I don't want some nosey hourly guy getting to them before we know what they are about. Tom no outside help this time. This is our baby."

After we got our baby locked away, we sent the children home for the weekend. They all had their schedules, duty rosters and blue and gray Kelly Security Uniforms.

Bruiser had the first ride in the booth that night and I was free until morning. A long "Hollywood" in one of the Bunkrooms three showers, washed away the last couple of days completely.

I slipped into the comfortable old Jeans and T-shirt Bailey had been thoughtful enough to bring me and headed out to the pool and the welcome smell of Pizza.

We sat and ate our slices without a lot of talk. The seven of us remembered the previous night and were recharging our batteries for another if necessary.

After awhile, we kinda drifted off our own ways. I went back to the bunkroom and laid on the only of the three units that wasn't a double-decker. I was staring at the ceiling, thinking, when it dawned on me. The other thing we found in the hole. It was all the dust. *"The floor wasn't dirt, just dirty."*

I was broken out of my revelation by Bailey. She had changed into a pair of gray sweats with NAVY across the front in blue. They looked a lot like the ones I kept on a shelf in my closet. What the hell, they never looked that good on me.

She stretched out on the cot next to me. We never said a word. Just a really good kiss goodnight and then blissful sleep.

If anything happened that night I wasn't told about it. I have to assume nothing did.

July 31

About the time the sun started to make it run over Lookout Mountain, the four of us had a loose grasp on one of the things Englewood was doing back in the forties. Our grasp was loose because there were never any names mentioned, just observer's initials and subject numbers. The tests conducted, as well as methods were also coded. I was sure the keys to those codes were in this building somewhere.

What we did know was that Englewood Facility had been conducting experiments on live humans. From the looks of these "behavior reports" some of these were really screwed up. "Subject 271 responds to stimuli x47 by attempting to force his body between the bars and yelling profanities." "Post mortem shows cause of death subject 219 to be successful self removal of the heart. Approximately 15 minutes after injection of L47."

We read several thousands of pages just like these. We had scanned about a third of the files over night. We did pause at the usual time for the local 12:21. The bell was beginning to take its toll.

About 0700 Bruiser told me he "had the booth" and since the bunkroom was now empty we all headed that way. We all opted for a quick shower before calling it a morning.

Hank and Shay being all but married anyway shared one leaving one each open for Bailey and me. I made mine quick and dressed in the last fresh set of clothes I had. *"Gonna have to make a trip to the house soon Bri."*

As I came out of the shower room Bailey

tossed me a pair of my sweats. I had several and from the looks of the ones she had on, she found most of them.

"Put those on they might be more comfortable to sleep in."

I changed right there and let her see me in my BVDs. Innocent, as she may have been, she never looked away. Then we slid in next to each other and slept for what seemed like forever.

Gunner woke me about six.

"Chief we got some chow in there and we thought you might want some."

After we ate it appeared they had worked everything out. They had decided that I needed to be fresh in the morning for my meeting with the troops so I should go home.

Seeing that I had no valid argument Bailey and I loaded up her car and went to my place. We did some laundry, *how romantic*, and sat back on my bed drinking wine and talking until we fell asleep. *Very romantic* I wanted her then. Wanted her bad but I could wait, I would wait. She was worth it.

Interlude July 21, Present

Up until now I have given you the day to day mostly so you would know where we all stood. I gave you most of what happened during those first couple of weeks. One or two minor things might have been forgotten and there might have been a minor spooking I wasn't told about, but you got the best of it anyways,

Now, I have a few housekeeping points to make clear so you know. I owned seventy percent of the company. I let the other nine of them buy in thirty percent and they pooled the money together and did it. I didn't know how they split that up and it didn't matter to me.

My thinking was if anyone wanted out, I would pay him or her five-percent of the company net worth at the time and that would be that. I guessed, then I would give the group the chance to buy that five-percent back. Way it was supposed to work was we agreed to split profits, after a twenty-percent growth reinvestment, seventy-thirty. How they split up the thirty, was up to them.

They had a partnership drawn up and it explained how it was all supposed to work. It didn't concern me then and still doesn't. I own seventy percent, the partnership, now adjusted, owns thirty.

They way it actually work for those first few months was all our income went into the account and the bills were paid out of that. If anything was left it stayed there until next time.

As for spending money I wrote each of them a check, for one thousand dollars, every Friday on my personal account.

Just a couple of more things before I get back to it. In addition to the guards and dispatchers I already told you about we also hired four salespeople and six alarm techs.

We also went and got six new Dodge Dakota pick-ups for them to use. Having damn near a million in your account sure doesn't hurt your line of credit any. I didn't get to know hardly any of their names I just wish I could say it was because I was to busy.

Finally I have to tell you that not once in that two weeks, or the three that followed, did we cut a single blade of grass. Nature still rules some things. Also we hired a cleaning crew but about all they did was empty trashcans. We never even changed a single light bulb.

Well I think that about brings you up to speed. So lets move on shall we.

Part 2 Open for Business (Ten Years Earlier)

August 1

I got to the office just a little before nine that morning. I walked into the pool to face the entire company. I was wearing a coat and tie that day, because I had to look like the boss.

Someone had set up a bunch of folding chairs facing a podium in front of the booth. Shay was standing at that podium just then talking to the staff. When I walked in she asked if I was ready. I wasn't really, but I nodded anyway.

I addressed the entire staff of Kelly Security that morning, including the admin temps.

I told them a lot of things. An excerpt from the speech follows.

"*Now with all of the pleasantries aside I have a few things I feel every member of this family should know. Up until about two weeks ago this building sat empty for about fifty years. The last purpose we know it served was as a research facility during WWII. We don't know much about it at this point, but from what we have been able to find out, they did some pretty nasty experiments here. Now why am I telling you this? Because, over the last two weeks, the rest of the management team and I, have seen some pretty strange things here. On at least one occasion furniture has been seen to move on it's own. What I am trying to tell you is, this building may or may not be haunted. What you choose to believe is completely up to you, but I feel each of you has a right to know. So far no one has been anything other than a little scared. However, we plan on taking no chances. Therefore, we have sat down a new policy that isn't in your employee handbook.*

At all times a member of management will be in this building, twenty-four hours a day seven days a week. There will be a roster posted with the duty manager's schedule. One of the upstairs offices will be converted into The Duty Managers Room. If you see anything that looks even remotely wrong, notify the duty Manager, or any member of the management team, immediately. At no time will anyone be alone in this building for any reason. No employee of this company is allowed to be in the bay after 1800 without a member of management present.

You will notice that a video monitoring system is being installed today in the pool, bay, upstairs hallway and rear drive area. This is not being done to keep an eye on you people; this is simply what "I" feel to be a necessary security measure.

No matter how silly you feel about

something you might see or hear in this facility, if it bothers you in any way, bring it to the attention of any manager. We are all available to you regardless of which department you work in. If for any reason one of my managers doesn't want to hear what you have to say, come and find me. My office is always open. If you have any questions about any of this, just ask a manager. One of us will try to find the answers. Lastly, if any of you feel uncomfortable enough not to work here I will completely understand. Now lets get out there and make things happen."

"I'd like to see all managers in the break room in a half an hour."

I then went to my office. I figured I'd give it some time and see how many new people my speech cost us.

From my office, I could hear and see service trucks and patrol units pulling out of the drive. Followed by, some of the sales force.

I knew we had four more new clients scheduled to go active today, projection showed we would have a total of sixteen active accounts by the end of the week. Everything else aside we were open for business; Jacob, A-21 and everything else be-damned. We would definitely need more staff and soon.

I walked into the break room for the first official staff meeting. They all looked like pros. Shay and Bailey had given up their jeans for gray skirts and white cotton blouses. They matched right down to the black soft-soled shoes. If memory serves me, and I am sure it does, they had a matching wardrobe and dressed alike for several months. Still do on occasion.

The sales guys were dressed like me; the rest were wearing the uniforms of their respective departments.

"Well, did we lose anyone yet?"

Heads were shook but nobody said anything.

I guessed this was a good thing.

"Ok then," I wanted to get what I had to say out then I'd let them have their say. "Ice, I want those cameras up today and the ability to monitor and record in dispatch. Along that note, I want to look into turning that booth into a double. We are going to have to eventually anyway." (We now have four separate monitoring facilities that run from Tulsa to OK City).

"Ken, look into getting that room set up upstairs so the Duty manager can have a little privacy. Also I want to have a couple of walls removed between some of the offices upstairs. One for your sales pit and the other for a conference room. This is the last weekly staff meeting we have in here.

"Bailey, keep a running recruitment ad in the world. Tom, ask around and see if you can get us some retired police cruisers, as many as you can, I want to increase our fleet. Ice, I want to hire some more experienced installers, pay em extra if they have their own trucks. Get with Bailey and make sure it gets in the ad. Ok, let's have it."

Ice was first. "Nobody quit on us and I was surprised by it to be truthful. I was wondering if anyone had any objections to me putting that old truck in service? I'd kinda like to use it as my service truck."

I thought a minute. "Bailey?"

"Well, by the time he gets it ready, it should be legal."

"Ok then, fine by me, just cover up the old lettering and decal it up. While we are at it let's get that ambulance painted in our color scheme and decaled up as well. We might park it out front or something. And let's get a light bar and decals on the Caddy to, but don't paint it."

That was all anyone had for me, which was good because two trucks from our suppliers were backing up to the loading dock and everyone but Bailey and I was on the working party.

I went back to my office to tackle some paperwork. I had gotten so involved in what I was doing; I grabbed the phone on the first ring. It was that same voice from a million miles away.

"You need to leave well enough alone!"
"Some things should stay buried."

There was No click, just a dial tone. I put the phone back on its cradle and pushed back from my desk. Something was getting ready to happen. I could feel it all over.

I had decided to start carrying my nine in a shoulder holster that morning. It had a comfortable feel to it at that moment in time.

I walked out the side door and was heading to the back lot. I noticed one of our Security People in the "Designated Smoking Area," it looked more like a bus stop, just lighting up. He was just a kid; still had the spackling of youth on his face.

I walked over just to be sociable. "Got another one of those?" It had been five years since I gave em up, but right now, that old familiar friend was calling to me.

"Sure thing sir," he was surprised and just a little intimidated by "The Boss" in such a casual environment.

I lit the Winston 100 he gave me with his lighter and inhaled deep with pleasure.

"What's your name kid?"

"David Morgan sir."

I could tell he would rather remain anonymous. Like most people new to a job, he felt better if the big guy didn't know who he was.

"Well, thanks David," I told him.

I continued my walk to the back. An old friend back in hand. Bailey was known to have a light from time to time, so I figured she wouldn't mind too much.

I leaned against the drive through overhead to finish my smoke. I was thinking I was gonna have to run down to the Circle K and get a pack of my own.

At first, I thought I was light headed from the smoke, because the door seemed have moved. Not up or down more like out. The second time, however, left me with no doubt. The door swelled out from the center like it was pregnant and it was creaking loudly.

I moved quickly, stepping aside, towards the loading dock. I almost wasn't fast enough. I was close enough to feel the wind as that door blew out and flew a hundred or so yards. It slammed into Garage one, hard enough to crack some of the cinder blocks.

All the overheads on the dock were open, so don't even think about negative pressure.

The guys had been in the bay, still unloading the trucks and putting the equipment away. Now they came running, sidearms in hand. David from the smoke hole came to. He was just curious; his gun was still strapped down.

"Put those things away;" I yelled. "Isn't anything here to shoot anyway."

"What the hell happened?" Bruiser had posed the question.

"A warning, I think."

"What kinda warning?"

"To keep our noses outta Foundation business I think." I told them about my phone call.

"So what are we gonna do about that door?" Ice asked being practical.

"Get those cameras up and call someone to fix it." Get a couple of guys to clean up that stuff around the garage. They can stack it in back for now."

I hadn't seen Bailey come through the bay, but I heard her ask if I was ok. She wasn't exactly looking at me, but more at the Winston still in my hand.

Most of the stuff I had asked for got done that day, in spite of everything that had happened. The cameras were up everywhere but the upstairs hall. The bunkroom upstairs had been set up. The end walls were gone from the booth and they had started on the one upstairs.

Since Ice had the Con, I figured I'd call it a day about six-thirty. I was gonna go over to Hank's place and have dinner with him, Shay and Bailey. I stopped off and picked up a pack of Doral 100's on the way.

After dinner we shot the shit a bit and then I headed home. Ice called me about 12:30 to tell me about a noise out back.

"There's nothing on the cameras chief and I

didn't see anything. I just thought you should know." I thanked him for the call and went back to sleep.

August 2 & 3

I threw my stuff and a change of clothes in
the car. Tonight was my turn in the duty room.
Figured it should be worlds of fun.

I had a funny feeling hit me as I pulled
through the gate. For some reason I felt
compelled to drive around back. I wasn't
disappointed.

That big overhead door was right back where
it had been yesterday at this time. Right where
it was when I leaned against it. No big surprise
either that the cracks were gone from the blocks
in the garage. *Must have been that negative
pressure again.*

I parked in the rear and walked around to the
side entrance, finishing my smoke. I was
pretty early so the only ones in the pool were

Ice and a couple of the night patrol guys.

"Hey chief," Ice greeted me. "You notice the back, did you? I saw it not long after I called ya last night." "Video shows it, not there one minute, there the next."

"Well guess we can cancel the repairman now. How'd the rest of the night go?"

"Aside from the little noise, which I probably only heard cause that damn phone woke me and I was sleeping right on top of it, real nice and quiet."

"Great, if you want to go get some chow or something go ahead."

"Nah, I'm good, Shawn's picking me up something from the McShack. You want something? I can get him on his cell."

"Thanks, but I grabbed a bagel at the QT on the way in."

"Ok then, there's a fresh pot in the booth

and the big one just got going in the break
room."

I detoured to the booth and got a cup. I
took my coffee upstairs and dropped my shit in
the duty room. Now that place was as about as
military as any duty room I had ever been in.

Ice had already stripped the rack and
tossed his linens in the hamper to the side. Hell
he had even laid out fresh stuff for me. Old
habits die-hard.

I hung my stuff on the bar and tossed my
bag next to the bed. I took the short walk to my
office. I was about halfway through the short
stack of papers in my "IN" box, when Bailey, Shay
and Hank joined me with a fresh cup of Joe.

The skirts were blue and their shirts were
almost a lemon color, but they were still twins.

"Hey boss" Bailey said sweetly.

"Yeah, morning chief" Shay chimed in.

Hank just gave the "howsitgoin" head bob. What he said was. "Nice job on the door. I didn't know the repair guys worked nights."

By the way he was smiling, I could tell he had heard Ice's story.

"Yeah apparently they do block work too and cover it with fifty year old, never fuckin fade paint, on top of everything else."

The look on their faces told me none of them had noticed that part. There was an awkward silence, followed by hank saying.

"Well Shay and me gotta run downtown with Tom to meet with the 911 People."

"You and I," Bailey added "have a meeting with the lawyer, here, in about 15 minutes."

"Well," I said, "guess we are all gonna be bored to tears for a little while. Might need more coffee."

Bailey gave me a smile "Gets even better,

after the lawyers, then we meet with the employee benefit people and the folks from Blue Cross."

I groaned. "Get out dragon lady and take your boring meetings with you."

Hank and Shay left, Bailey stayed. She moved my papers from the desk to the in box and replaced them with, well, her.

"Would you care for some company tonight?"

"Love it," I answered, maybe too fast.

"Good," she said hopping off the desk. "Cause that obligates you to be here with me Thursday."

She turned and smiled at me from the office door. I would have married her then and there.

"Wouldn't miss it for anything." I sipped my coffee and hurried through my short stack.

The meeting with the lawyers went pretty well. They did most of the talking. Bailey did most of the listening. I pretended to care. It did, however, go a little long, *they are lawyers, what did you expect Bri they bill by the hour.* So by the time they left the Benefits people were waiting.

I excused myself to run refresh my Java from the pot in the admin office and was back with them. Only had one problem this time. I had to pay attention.

That meeting went mostly good as well. Right up until 12:21. I guess she didn't want to look foolish in front of our guests, so Bailey picked it up.

"Kelly Security."

As she listened, I watched her light olive complexion go to light ashen. She slammed the receiver down on my desk and ran out of the office without so much as an excuse me. I put it to my ear and I heard that million-mile voice laughing insanely.

I hung it up and looked at my visitors.

"Folks, you are going to have to excuse us for a bit. Why don't you go down those back stairs, to the break room, and have some coffee or a soda. We will be back with you shortly."

I didn't wait for an answer. I had that; "something's going to happen," feeling again. I bolted out the office and straight through the door marked ladies, where Bailey was splashing her face with water and trying not to cry.

It was obvious what ever she had for breakfast was no longer with her. I decided to get her out of there, before one of our female guests decided a trip to the powder room was in order, before, refreshments.

I led her down the front steps, pausing at the door long enough to yell t the dispatcher.

"Find Mr. Fox for me now."

I took her outside and across the back

drive to the fence. Her color hadn't come back yet and she was shaking something terrible. I was holding her up, because she couldn't do it on her own.

Finally she sat down on the grass and leaned against the fence. She had grabbed her purse on the way out of my office, a woman's instinct, and was fishing her smokes out, still not speaking. I figured she had the right idea so I grabbed one of mine and lit both of them. About this time Ken found us.

"What the hell boss, you alright? The dispatcher was hollering something about Miss Kirk…"

He stopped when he looked at her. Bailey was like a daughter to Ken and he was a great father. He sat down next to her, putting his arm around her shoulder.

"You alright hun, cause you're not looking well."

I told him what little I knew and added, "just give her some time."

She pulled us both a little closer and looked in my eyes. I could see her pain.

"He asked me if I had enjoyed my reading lately." She took a deep breath. "Then he told me that report left something out, the guy not only removed his own heart, but he ate it before he died. He said, he could show me how too."

She went back silent and lowered her head. A thought was forming in my head but not taking shape. It did about the time Ken picked up his radio.

"Base 1-1."

"Go 1-1."

"Base 0-0 has visitors, I need you to get them out of the building ASAP."

"Roger 1-1, anything else?"

"10-4 base I need any level ones you can find."

"Copy 1-1, Stand by" O

Our weekday dispatcher was experienced and she was sharp. She did three simple things that accomplished more than what we wanted but exactly what we needed. It wasn't by design, but it worked.

First she threw the switch that disconnected us from 911, Great for fire drills, then she activated our fire alarm and finally she pushed the panic button. The later was obvious when our pagers went off.

She followed every rule, no one in the building alone. She came out right with everyone else.

Ice had been in the booth, doing the modifications I asked for. He made sure the insurance people went out the new fire exit on the other side. He told me later, he put them in their cars and told them we would reschedule. He didn't remember if he told them who he was.

All of management was in the building except Shay and Hank, who had gone to lunch. I had no doubt they would be here soon.

When our fire alarm goes active our phones automatically forward to a cell we keep in the booth. If that one is busy, it goes to Ice's phone. If he's tied up, mine is the next in line. The one from the booth rang. The dispatcher answered it and handed it to me.

"Chief this is Shay, what's going on?"

"Don't panic doll," I said, "Everything is under control, just get here as soon as you can."

"We are three mikes out chief and headed your way."

"Make that two."

I heard Hank in the background as she ended the call. What few hourly people, that were in the building, had gathered in the front lot like they were supposed to. I didn't want any of them wandering over in our direction. I sent Ken over to round them up and get ready to take them inside.

I had just started telling Ice to go back in with the dispatch and get us back to normal, as Hank's Vette swung in through the gate driving right to us. Just as he opened his door, the ground heaved beneath us.

It was a wave that ran the depth of the lot. It started at the fence, directly behind us, moving towards the building, then past it; fading away as it reached the far fence. It was repeated three times. Anyone that had been standing wasn't any longer.

The building never moved. Shook like hell but never moved. How could it move, it being on a six-inch slab? Those two garages were another, matter both of them had moved a total of six inches.

We were too busy to think or ask questions. A quick check told us no one was hurt at all. Not even any scratches or bruises. Everyone was a little scared, but that was all.

Those in the front lot had been thoughtful enough to bring their purses and keys with them, as people are apt to do when the fire alarm goes off. They were all sales and admin. Non-essentials so to speak, so I sent them home then and there. That just left us with dispatch.

"Guess it's over." I said. "Might as well go back in."

We went into the pool; Ice killed the alarm and got us back up. The operator did a systems check, then a Comm check with the guards. She had a hand held with her outside, but it was best to be safe. She was a pro.

The rest of us went to the far side of the pool for a quick get together. Bailey was still shaken and not talking. I broke a company rule and lit a smoke. Soon everyone that smoked joined me.

When Ice got done in the booth, and back with us, I told those that didn't already know about Bailey's phone call. Shay leaned over and hugged her tightly.

"Shit honey, you want me to take you home?"
"What do you think chief."

I looked at Bailey and she pulled me down close, so I could hear, and whispered "I ain't getting more then ten feet from you for the rest of the day Brian. Got that Brian?"

I got it and even though she had whispered, everyone else got it too.

"Settles that." I said. "Guys have a look around and give me a damage report. I'll be right here, with Bailey, until she gets to feeling better."

They all headed out.

"Shannon." Bailey's voice had more strength, but she was still using full names. "You stay awhile too, OK?"

"Sure thing baby, anything you want."

We sat in silence smoking now and then and drinking a lot of coffee. Bailey smoked more that day, then I had seen her smoke in a month. What the hell, I couldn't blame her. The only minor problem came, when I had to get rid of about a gallon of that coffee.

Bailey wanted to stay true to the word about the ten-foot rule. Now, I love her to death; I'll be the first to admit it, but I just wasn't ready for her to watch me taking a whiz. Hell, I was married six years the first time and I didn't like her watching.

Ended up her and Shay stood by the door. I was hoping it wasn't more than ten feet from there to the pisser. Hell, I wanted her happy.

Soon everyone was coming back with minor damage reports. Cracked window here or a stuck door there. Worst thing was those garages. I figured they'd be all right. Probably fixed by morning. Of that I was sure. All of it would, I was willing to bet big on it.

The only casualty so far, was a coffee cup my CO gave me when I made E-7. It was laying on the desk in front of us in about fifteen pieces. I never drank coffee out of it, but it had some meaning to me anyway. Bailey picked up several pieces and started making like to put it back together. She had a tear on her cheek.

Just then Ice, who had been in the bay with Shawn, came running back into the pool. He was breathing hard and in a panic. *Guess we're gonna have to change your name buddy."*

"Chief, I need everyone in the bay, quick! The chains broken on that trap door and it's standing open."

We all jumped up and headed for the bay.

"Ice, where the hells Shawn?" I hollered over my shoulder.

"That's the other thing, he's just standing there staring at that hole, not moving."

By then I saw him. And it was just like Ice said. We all kinda gathered around him and the hole.

"Bruiser, give me a hand with this thing."

We each grabbed a side of the door and slammed them shut. Just before they closed completely two things happened.

First, I saw and felt something come out of that hole. It was like a slight shimmer and something touching my arm.

The other thing, I caught a glimpse of a shiny black phone. It looked real familiar.

That shimmer was headed right for Shawn,

but Bailey, not looking, stepped right between them. We all saw it but there was nothing we could do. Damn thing went right through her and him too. Straight out the back of the bay. It showed up even better on the tape from the security cameras, when we watched them later.

Shay and I raced to Bailey, while Ice jumped to his brother's side. I grabbed her and spun her around, to make sure she was all right. I hit my knees in shock. Her hair, about a half-inch on either side of her face had gone white.

"Bailey, you ok?" "My God are you ok?" She smiled and put her hand on my shoulder.

"Feeling a little better now Bri." She said. "Bri, Honey what's wrong?"

Shay, correctly figuring she was better at this than I was, took over quick.

"Honey I like the look on you." "I have never seen highlights that good come out of any beauty shop."

Bailey lifted the hair on one side of her face, looked at it, then at me. Then Fainted into my arms.

Shawn hadn't faired any better. Bailey had caught mostly a glancing blow but he took it full on. His hair had gone completely white! He looked more like the older brother now. Aside from the visual difference he fine. Was even talking and joking with his brother and Gunner. He seemed ok, but different.

I carried Bailey back inside, straight to the bunkroom. The rest of them started to follow. I turned to Ken.

"Hey man, how about you, Gunner and Tom, see if you can get another chain on that thing."

He nodded and they headed off. Bruiser stopped me and nodded to the booth.

"I know she saw all that shit chief." I'm gonna go make sure she's ok. I'll get that tape."

If I didn't know better (which I didn't') I would have thought he was getting a little sweet on her (Which he was).

"Sure Bruiser, take your time." He headed off in that direction.

In the fresh light of the break room, I looked at Bailey, lying on the couch, with her cousin and Shay hovering over her. If it was possible, she had gotten even more beautiful.

After a few minuets she opened her eyes and sat up. She looked a little tired and a little shaken but otherwise fine. She smiled at me and gave me a puzzled look.

"Bri, what happened to *your!* Hair?"

I looked in the mirror over the sink, I saw that I too had gone white, just at the temples.

"Must have happened when, whatever the fuck that thing was, brushed my arm on it's way out. The cold wasn't just cold it was fear."

"That's about the way I feel about it too,"
Bailey added softly.

Then Shawn finished "Yeah, me too."

About the time the chain gang joined us.
Shift change was going on in the pool.

"Lets move this to my office." I offered.
Everyone agreed, or at least they didn't argue.

We headed up, Bruiser hurrying to catch us.

"She didn't see it chief. She was busy with
the radio. But its all there, by Gawd, on that
fuckin tape, every bit of it."

I put the tape in the VCR, in my office,
and we all watched. The cameras in the bay are
motion activated, so they come on when anything
moves. Each one has it's own recorder. Bruiser
had gotten all three of them for the bay as well
as the one from the pool recorder.

The Bay cameras activated when the waves
started. The only things that moved in the bay

were those doors on the hole and that's where the cameras focused their attention. We were watching the feed from the camera on the front center wall of the bay.

It had zoomed in on the doors. They slammed against the chains with each wave. On the last wave, the chain broke and the doors flew open. Then a blip, as motion stopped and the camera went back to standby. Then the doors again.

The camera sweeps to the end of the bay as Ice and Shawn came in. The scene follows their progress until they stop near the open doors. We follow Ice as he runs to get us. A blip and then we come out into the bay. *Shawn never moved, not once the whole time.*

It follows us to the hole. We watch as Bruiser and I shut the doors. The camera catches the shimmer and we see it brush through my arm, catch about four inches of Bailey's side and slam right through Shawn.

The other two tapes show different angles of the same silent movie.

Shawn asked, "Where the hell did I go? I remember walking up to the hole man, then, that's it until I see you guys all over and Bailey's falling. I don't remember anything else. I swear to ya chief, I don't."

"Take it easy Shawn," I said. "Shit like that happens all the time. Don't dwell on it."

Bruiser changed the subject. "Now here's one you're really gonna love."

He put in the tape from the pool recorder. This camera is a slow feed. Takes one frame every five seconds. Saves tape. However, when the fire or security alarms are activated it goes into normal film mode. Because of this, we were able to see the shaking of the building with each wave but that really wasn't important.

What was important, happened about ten seconds after the last wave. We had to rewind the tape twice for everyone to catch it, but you really couldn't miss it. The Cabinet with the chains, it was there one second, gone the next.

"I checked after I looked at this Chief," Bruiser offered. "It's fuckin gone."

It hit me then. The phone I glimpsed as we shut the doors was sitting on that cabinet, the one with the chains. I told them about that and then we just sit in silence.

After a few minutes I said, "you guys might as well get home. Bailey and I are gonna be here. If anything else happens I'll let you know."

Hank says "Shay and I are gonna stick it out here with you, if you don't mind."

"Not at all," I answered thankfully. "But you gotta go grab us some chow first. Tomorrow, we'll go have another look in the hole."

"I really don't think that would be a good Idea Jacob"

My skin crawled and Bailey lost her color again. It was Shawn talking, but the voice was the one from the phone. I looked dead at him.

"And just why the hell is that?" I demanded.

"What, huh, cause the thought of it gives my the creeps. That's why."

The voice was his that time and I let it go. As we all left my office, I reached over and took the black bastard off the hook. Didn't know how much good it would do, but I would in about three hours.

Everyone headed home. Shay and Hank headed to Arby's to get us some Beef-n-Cheddar's. Bailey and I sat on the couch in the break room.

I was holding her close and trying to make sense of the day.

"Bri, it was him." "The guy from the phone, it was him talking through Shawn."

"It sure sounded like it to me Babe." I just held her a little tighter.

Ten minutes later we were eating and talking with Hank and Shay. Bailey was doing much better now. You could tell by her voice, more importantly the glow was back in her face and the shine back in her eyes. She was going to be ok.

They had made a run by their place and picked up an overnight bag, which told me they planned on staying. This was just fine with me. We had intentionally put two double beds in the duty room for just such emergencies.

I waited until the four of us were up there, to tell them what had Bailey and I so bothered.

"You sure about that chief?" Shay asked. "Cause that's about as fucked up as things have ever gotten around here."

Bailey answered her. "Positive Shay." "I will *never* forget that voice."

Hank asked me, "what do you plan to do about it chief."

"Nothing, for now. Let's just wait and see." Then a different plan hit me. "Bailey, what do we have going tomorrow?"

"Just routine Bri, what ever the fuck that means." "Why?"

"Hank, think you can handle things here?"

"Sure, chief. What you got in mind?"

"Nothing, just gonna take the day off and I'm taking Bailey with me."

They were all looking at me like I was out of my mind.

"Honest guys, we will be at my place the whole time."

"Well alright then." Shay winked. "Boss man and his sweetie playin hooky."

Bailey giggled. "Cool."

We all drifted off to sleep and the phone woke us right on time. "*Damn black son of a bitch in there ringing and it ain't even on the fuckin hook. Hell you ain't hooked up to nothing, well maybe hell!*"

We let it ring and it gave up. After that, we could hear what had to be the garages sliding back in place.

One look, in the back, the next morning confirmed that. Just like I suspected. All damage to the building or grounds had vanished overnight. All but my cup and Bailey had that in her bag.

I told the guys my plan and Bailey and I headed to my place and twenty-four hours away from hell house.

I cooked us breakfast while she soaked in my garden tub. About the time it was ready, she came out wearing one of my old t-shirts and looking absolutely wonderful.

We ate in the den, snuggled up in my leather loveseat. We stayed there for a long time, not saying a word. I was very tired and knew she had to be completely exhausted.

After about an hour I suggested sleep and she was all for it. I stripped down to nothing but an old pair of navy shorts and we cuddled up in my king size bed. We just held each other kissing now and then when we felt the need. At one point I brushed her hair back from her face and said frankly.

"I Love You Bailey Kirkwood!"

She smiled sweetly. "Well Brian Kelly. I love you too."

She kissed me again and leaned over to turn out the lamp on her side of the bed. And I saw the name on that back of my old softball T-shirt B. Kelly. It was on her, but it worked for me.

August 4

We slept the rest of that day and well into the night. The phone call at 12:40 pulled me out of a dreamless bliss.

It was Bruiser; he was taking his turn on duty. He sounded excited and out of breath.

"Chief, you better get down here now. The dispatcher left, to be honest, I'm thinkin of doin' the same."

I tried to calm him. "Bruiser, what's going on?" Are you there alone?"

"Shit man, I switched everything to auto. I'm in the van, with the cell and the radio." I got a couple of patrol guys here with me. Chief, Shawn is here too, he's inside, but that's part of the problem."

I was getting dressed while I was listening.

"I'll be there in five minuets. Call Hank and fill him in." Have him drop Shay here, to stay with Bailey."

I hung up and grabbed my keys. Bailey called out sleepily.

"Bri, what's going on?"

I kissed her on the forehead. "Stay here, Shay will be here in a bit. I'll call you when I figure it out."

I left her with just that and no more. Whatever was going on, I didn't want her to be a part of. She'd had enough.

I pulled into the lot four minuets later, parking the Ramcharger next to the van. Bruiser jumped out of the driver's side to meet me. Every light in the building was on. I may have imagined it, but they seemed to be brighter than normal.

"Let's have it Bruiser."

"Chief, about 00:15, I was in the break room having some coffee and reviewing some reports. I hear the dispatcher say 'Good evening Mr. Poole.'" I look up to see Shawn standing there looking around the pool, like he forgot something."

"Then that damn phone up in your office starts ringin'. Shawn gets this look, like he figured out the secrets of the universe or somethin. Then he starts moving shit around. Chief, I mean the shit that was already here before we came. Like he was puttin' it back or somethin'."

"I tried to stop him, I swear chief, but he threw me against the wall from the middle of the room. That's about when the dispatcher took off, ain't seen him since."

"I went back at him chief, but he got some damn super strength, like he's on Angel Dust or somethin'."

"I went to the booth, called a unit in for back-up, then grabbed the cell and a hand-held and threw the switch. That's when I called you."

I took a minute to digest it all. This was just too much.

"Ok." "Bruiser did you call hank?"

"Yea Chief, called his brother too. They are both on their way. Chief, Ice says he's been looking for Shawn. Said he walked out about 23:30 without a word."

After a minute I said, "Bruiser I'm gonna go find out what Shawn's up to."

He grabbed my arm. "Hell you are! Brian, with all due respect, I'm bigger'n you and he through my ass around like I was a fluff filled teddy bear. I think you need to wait for Hank and Ice." I didn't have to wait long.

With in seconds of each other, Hank and Ice

pulled in. It took Bruiser and I both to keep Ice from just charging in the building. I turned him to face me.

"Hold on Ice, we go together."

"Chief, what the hells going on with Shawn?"

"Let's go find out."

As we headed towards the door, I noticed the patrol guys were coming too.

"You guys wait here. Mind the radio. See if you can get Gunner."

I heard one of them ask, "Who the hell's Gunner?" I'd let him figure that out.

What I felt when I opened the door was not surprise, but a perfect mixture of shock and horror. Everything we hadn't gotten rid of, that was in the building before we moved in, was right back where it had been.

Evidently things didn't exactly match up. It was a scary sight. There were desks without typewriters and typewriters without desks. Just hanging there as if the desk was invisible. He must have moved fast, or had help, because there was shit in the pool that had been moved upstairs or, out in the bay. One desk had been stuck halfway through the break room wall, like something out of the Philadelphia Experiment.

Boxes of personal stuff were sitting against the back wall. I was particularly drawn to a black sweater, hanging on the back of a non-existent chair. Shawn was at the far end, emptying a box into invisible drawers, of an invisible desk.

"What the fuck Shawn?" Ice yelled.

At the sound of his brother's voice, Shawn looked up. He dropped a bracelet he was holding, onto the top of the invisible desk. The bracelet hovered for a second, then fell to the floor, as did everything else. My blood ran ice cold.

"Sup Steve?" Shawn said, apparently amazed by where he was. He looked around the pool and said. "What the fuck happened here?" He looked at Ice kinda funny. "Man, one minute I'm goin' to bed, next minute I'm here in the pool surrounded by all this shit. What the fucks goin on Steve!" He started to cry.

I whispered to Ice, "man, get him outta here quick."

As Ice led his brother outside, I looked at Hank and Bruiser, who were looking to me for an answer. Evidently, the patrol guy had figured out who Gunner was, cause I damn near jumped out of my skin when he called me on my cell.

"Chief, man, what the fucks goin on. Dumb ass guard callin' me, sayin' shit about furniture needin' to be moved or some shit."

"Gunner, everything is under control," I lied. "Call Ken and Tom, I need you guys to meet us at the office."

"More weird shit man?"

"Yeah, I sighed, "but come on just the same, ok?"

"Got it boss, on our way."

I hung up with gunner and called Bailey at my place.

"Bri, what is it?" "Everything ok?"

"Bailey, Everything's fine." I lied again. "We just got a mess to clean up. Listen, I don't want you to come to work tomorrow."

"Hey, to hell with that Bri…"

I cut her off. "Bailey, please listen to me." "I want you and Shay to start looking for another location. Find one fast."

"Bri, what the hell's going on?"

"Look Bailey, I've had all this place I can stand. We will run things here, until we get set up somewhere else. Then, we'll write this son of a bitch off as a loss. When you find something, call me. What ever you do, I don't want you to come back here!"

I looked at Hank and Bruiser, "anyone want to check the bay with me?" They didn't want to, but we did anyway.

Things in there were just as I suspected. The chain had been broken again, but the doors were closed. All of our stuff had been moved back into the bay and the cages were open, all but A-21.

We just stood there for while, not believing what we saw. No one spoke. I don't remember even breathing.

After awhile I said, "Let's go check on Shawn." They didn't argue.

Outside in the warm August air I felt better. I was still tired and scared, but now I was pissed. Now this thing was fuckin with people

I cared about. Making them do weird shit. I thought of Bailey. I couldn't let things get any worse.

Ice and Shawn were sitting on the edge of the open side door of the van. Shawn started to say something, but I stopped him.

"It's ok kid. Just let it go for now."

I lit a smoke and leaned against the Ramcharger. We hung out in silence and waited for the others.

It took them about ten more minutes. They all came together in Gunners Cherokee. I filled them in on everything I knew and stood back looking at their disbelieving faces.

"That's some wicked shit chief," Gunner said, shaking his head.

"Sure enough," Ken almost laughed, "shoulda called this place the Amityville Foundation."

Tom stared past me at Shawn. "I know I'm

the new guy, but something's wrong with that kid. I thought so all along, but more so now, since, whatever the fuck that was went through him in the bay.

I had to agree with him, worse, I didn't see things getting any better.

"Guys, let's try and get things looking presentable. Cause short of the Titanic pulling up to the loading dock, we still have a business to run. Ice, why don't you take your brother home. Try to keep him there this time"

By the time we got the pool half ass straight, the sun was up and people were showing up for work. Hank and I had gathered all the shit from the admin office and loaded it in the vans.

I didn't want those girls there either. I gave them directions to my place. Then I told dispatch to forward all admin calls there. I called Bailey and told her they were coming. I was in no mood to argue about things. I hung up without giving her the chance.

After brushing off the woman I loved, I took my coffee, Hank and Ken to my office. I knew we had to do something. I needed a plan.

I told then my intentions on finding a new location. Ken seemed all right with it. Hank, much to my surprise, was a different story. His look scared me, his words even more so.

"Well I'll be damned, I never thought I would see the day when bad ass Chief Brian Kelly gave up. That's what you're doin', givin' up. Just gonna let this thing beat you, is that it?"

I was in shock. "Hank, god damn it, haven't you been paying attention? This ain't some power hungry Dictator or a homicidal Colombian Drug Lord we're dealing with. Fuck man, I don't know what in the hell we're dealing with here and neither do you."

"What I do know, is I've got a kid out there that may never be the same. I have to carry that load and still face his brother every day. I also I have a responsibility to make sure nobody else gets fucked up like that. So if that's givin' up, I guess I am."

Hank started to say something, but Ken stopped him. He said calmly, "Hank, I know what your feeling, I feel it too. This place was a dream come true for all of us man, but it ain't dyin. It's just changing location."

I think more would have been said, if my office phone, the real one, hadn't rang.

"Brian Kelly," I answered on the second ring.

"Don't talk just listen." The voice sounded old. "You don't know me, you don't wanna' know me and you aren't going to. I know what you're looking for and I can help you find it."

I looked at my caller ID; it said "Anonymous."

"The name you want is Jacob Harris. Most of the other stuff you can get from those rooms you're all afraid to go in. He gave a wheezing laugh. Never even opened them again did ya. Now all this will help you if you still want to find the answers. If it were me, I'd let it go. One more very important thing Mr. Kelly, all the months of the year start with a letter. You military people just like to call them a number now." He hung up.

I was just about to grab my keys and have a look in those rooms, when my other phone, the black one, rang. It wasn't even ten yet.

"Who the fuck is this?" I screamed into the phone.

"Now, now Jacob," the far off voice answered. "What kind of way is that to talk?"

"I'm not Jacob, you son of a bitch," I yelled back.

The voice on the other end of the phone

changed it became deep, hostile and hoarse, and my skin crawled.

"I know perfectly fucking well your not Jacob mother fucker. So just shut the fuck up and listen to me asshole. You stop fucking with stuff that don't belong to you and leave my facility now. I'll make you pay Bri, oh yeah, I'll make you *all* pay. Now quit looking for answers and GET THE FUCK OUT!"

"Bring it the fuck on BITCH!" I yelled and slammed the phone down.

I looked at Hank. "Ok, I'm not giving up, but we are going to move Operations and Admin somewhere else, for now."

"What's up chief?" Ken asked, looking confused.

"Mother Fucker called me Bri, now it's personal." "Come on." I grabbed my keys and they followed me out of the office.

I was planning on going straight to those offices. I changed my mind and went to the pool instead. I still didn't have a plan. Anything from this point was going to be on a volunteer only basis. They had to know everything I knew and make an informed decision.

I was going to get some answers, come hell or high water, but first, I had to get the innocents out of harms way.

I called Bailey. "Hey babe, how are things going with your search?"

"I found a couple of office suites, but I'm not sure if either of them is big enough."

"Can they handle Admin and Ops?"

"Probably, if we got them both but…"

"Secure them both ASAP" I cut her off. "Bri are you ok?"

"I'm good," not exactly a lie, "get going on it, I don't care what it costs. I want to move operations and Administration there as soon as we can."

"It will take a few days Boss, but I'll rush everything I can."

"I know you will Bailey. Until then, as long as someone is in this building I am here too. Keep your admin girls away. If you need anything, one of us will get it to you."

"Bri," she started but I cut her off.

"That's the way it has to be Bailey, no more questions."

"Ok Bri," she hesitated, "Brian I love you."

"I love you too Bailey." No matter what, I planned to prove that to her soon.

I told the guys about my two phone calls and waited for it to sink in. When none of them had anything to say I started talking.

"Way I see this, we can do one of two things. We can stick this out until we find another suitable location and then just walk away. Or, we can fight back. We can look for some answers. Who knows if we find the right piece of the puzzle, this thing just might go away. I, for one, at least want the answers."

"Listen guys, this is volunteer only, but if you're in, you do exactly as I say, no questions. What's it gonna be boys?"

Hank was first and a little too quick. "I'm in, let's get this fucker."

He still thinks it's something he can shoot. "Just let him keep it for now buddy."

"Me too," that was Ken.

Tom and Gunner nodded in agreement. Bruiser looked at each one of us and said.

"I'm with you guys, but you gotta know somethin first. That shit last night scared me.

Like nothin else ever has. I won't ever let any of you down chief, just want you all to know."

I put my hand on Bruisers shoulder. "Hell, any of you ain't scared, you better leave now, cause you ain't going to do any of us any good when you get that way."

I had to say it, but I knew they all were, at least a little.

"Well, I guess we're all in then."

Then Ken asked, "what about Ice and Shawn." "I'll have to talk to Ice, but as for Shawn well…"

Tom interrupted, "best to leave that one out of this for now. Chief keep him the hell away."

"Tom, I hope we can."

"What's the plan Chief?" Gunner asked.

"Not something we discuss in here," I

replied. Then I said to the dispatcher, "Set everything on auto, take the cell and the portable out to the van. Notify all you units base is off limits for now."

She gave me a weird look; but did it anyway. As soon as the dispatcher was clear I led them out of the building and to the other van.

"Get in," I said, "we'll talk in there."

Once the doors were closed I laid out my plan.

"First, no one is ever alone in any part of that building period. If you gotta piss, do it in pairs. Everyone has a radio on at all times. There are two places I consider hot zones, those four offices upstairs and the bay. If we got there, we do it in force. We go with no fewer than four people, and never without me."

"Tom, I want you to do some research. Use whatever contacts you got. I want to know everything you can find about Jacob Harris or

Englewood Foundation."

"Ken I would like to figure a way to get Dispatch out of the building. Any ideas?"

"Not that I can see," he answered." "We still have to monitor all the systems."

Tom smiled and said, "I got an idea chief, but I gotta make a call first."

"Ok, make the call."

Tom got out of the van and made a call on his cell. When he got back in his smile was bigger.

"Talked to a friend with Tulsa PD motor pool. The city just got a new mobile command post. They still have the old one. I saw it while I was down there, looking at some squad cars yesterday. It's ours on loan, no questions asked. We can even buy it later, if you want."

"Damn good work," I said, not believing our luck. "How soon can you get it here?"

"Soon as Gunner gets me over there, he's even gonna send over a couple of his guys to help us patch it in to our systems."

Ken added, "hell should be up in a couple of hours tops then."

"Ok," I said, "you two go, the rest of us will hang out in the pool and handle the booth until this gets online."

We exited the van. Tom left with Gunner in his Jeep. The rest of us went back to the pool. We couldn't convince the dispatcher to stay in the van. Bruiser never left her side.

It stayed pretty quiet the rest of the day. That didn't keep us from being on edge waiting to see what would happen next. About half an hour later, Tom and Gunner got back with our new command post.

The command post was a sweet setup. A converted greyhound type bus. It had a command center, complete with monitors and a sophisticated phone system, right behind the driver's seat. In the back was a small office with a table surrounded by six seats. It would work just fine.

Three hours later the converted bus was ready for action. You could have fought a war from in there. The cables only gave us a hundred feet, I hoped it would be enough.

Ken made sure everything was patched in from outside the building, better safe than sorry. All patrols were informed that everything would be done from the mobile post. I locked the doors to hell, since it was dark. Then I settled into the command post and called Ice.

He was pissed at being left out of the loop, but given the situation with Shawn he understood. I asked him to keep Shawn away for a little longer anyway and he agreed.

"He seems ok now, a little distant, but Hell chief find out what the fucks going on, OK?"

I promised I'd do my best and hung up.

Bruiser came to where we all were sitting in the back of the bus.

"Listen Chief, I think things are as safe here as they gonna get. All of you guys got people you need to talk to and set all this shit right with. Mandy, that's our day dispatcher, went to my place to pick up some things. Her and I will stay here and hold down the fort with the night guys."

"Bruiser," "Hank and I will be at my place, we're closest so call us first. Tom, you do your research in the morning and call me about noon."

"Got it chief."

"The rest of you go home. I suggest you tell your wives what's going on. Tell them everything. If we are going to do this, I want everyone that matters to know the whole game."

Hank and I went to my place and spelled everything out to Bailey and Shay. They raised holy hell about being "protected women" and thought they should be a part of it. In the end we all went to bed mad. Bailey in my bed, Shay in the guestroom, Hank on the sofa in the living room. I folded the hid-a-bed out of the loveseat in the den, which was now our admin office.

I stared at the ceiling for hours. Sleep wouldn't come. *"Tomorrow I will have some fucking answers no matter what.*

August 5

Bailey woke me at seven and said curtly, "there's coffee and some breakfast in the dinning room boss."

She walked away with nothing further. I found Hank, in the dining room, eating. The look on his face and the absence of Shay, led me to believe he had met with a similar attitude. He confirmed it for me.

"Damn man, why they gotta make such a big deal outta this shit."

"Got me Hank, but they have a point. We are being sexist. It doesn't change a fuckin thing, but it's true.

After we ate, I looked at him across the

table.

"You ready for this shit?" I asked.

"Hell no, but let's do it anyway." Then he added, "better try to make up a little first real quick." I nodded.

He went looking for Shay and I hunted Bailey down. I found her in the den.

"Look, I'm sorry and you're right. I know you're not happy with me. Maybe I'm being stubborn and foolish, but I can't protect you from whatever is going on in any way except keeping you away from it."

She stood and faced me with closed fists. "Who in the hell is going to protect you Brian?" She took a deep breath and continued. "I can almost understand you wanting to keep me away from it. In some twisted way, it's sweet, but I can't understand why you feel *you* have to keep at it. God, why can't you just let it go?"

I didn't answer. I couldn't answer. I just went to her but she turned away.

"Go chase your windmills, but by God you better come back."

Hank and I drove the five minutes to the office in silence. We were early, but so was everyone else.

Ken, Bruiser and Gunner were in the back of the bus, surrounding the coffeepot. Bruisers' Mandy was in the operations area, looking refreshed and doing her job.

Bruiser informed me the night had been real quiet. First "quiet" night I could remember. I got right down to business.

"First thing I think we need to do, is get in those offices upstairs and see what we can find. We stay together, no matter what happens."

"What exactly are we looking for chief?" Gunner asked.

"I don't know for sure guys, that's the honest truth." I replied. "But I think we'll know it when we see it. For sure anything about Jacob Harris, or A-21. I think that's the key to the whole thing."

"You think it's gonna be that easy chief?" Hank asked.

I answered honestly, "No, not at all. I think we need to be ready for anything."

"Anything," happened pretty damn fast. I opened the door to the pool and was immediately blown back out into the drive. I knocked Bruiser and Ken down on my way. They all ran to me, but I waved them off.

"Gonna have to do better than that." I told it.

I opened the door again this time I braced myself. I probably looked kind of foolish cause nothing happened.

The pool looked just like we had left it. For just a second I felt kinda silly. It was just a big room and that was all. Then I heard a door close upstairs and I remembered it wasn't just a room.

We went hurried to the noise without a word. We found nothing, not that I expected to. The place was silent as a church auction, except for our breathing.

"Guess the next move is ours boss." It was Ken.

"Let's make it then." I pulled out my keys.

My cell rang right then making all of us jump. "Yeah," I answered.

"Chief, it's Ice." "You ain't gonna believe this shit man. Shawn's gone again. Just fucking vanished."

"Get here soon, man."

"On my way."

I closed the phone and said, "Change of plans, Shawn's moving again, everybody out."

"Fucking building must've rolled a double." I'm not sure who said that.

Somehow whatever had this building had Shawn too. I put my need for an answer aside. People always come first. We had to find Shawn and keep him safe!

When we got to the pool, I had another thought. "Ken, where's the video feed from this place going?"

He thought for a second. "Still over there." He pointed to the booth.

"Let's check it out."

The monitors were still going. I switched through each of the cameras several times. Nothing was moving. Then I saw it. The white truck Ice had taken home to fix up. It was sitting in front of the double garage. Shawn must be here somewhere.

"Hank, you and Ken check out back. The rest of you stay with me, we'll check the building."

I ejected all the tapes from their recorders and handed them to Hank. "Drop these off in the bus."

They went out the side door and we started our search upstairs. We had done a room by room of the upstairs, for the second time that day I was about to unlock the first of the four "hot offices, when we heard a hell of a crash down in the pool.

"Hank," I yelled into the radio. "In the pool now, cover both doors."

We got to the bottom of the stairs about the time Hank and Ken were coming in the side doors. The pool was empty and smoke was coming from the booth.

The video monitors, about the only things

left in the booth, had been smashed. We all had our guns out and it made me uneasy.

"Put those away," I said holstering my own. "We can't shoot whatever this is and we sure as hell ain't gonna shoot Shawn."

"He's here somewhere chief," Hank said.

"I know he's here, but where?"

In unison, we all looked at the door to the bay. We had walked right past it. It was open.

"Bruiser, you go out to the bus with Mandy. Just in case. I guess the rest of us are going the check the bay."

He nodded and left in a hurry. I gave him a full minute and then keyed the radio.

"Bruiser, sit rep."

"All secure here chief, five by five."

"Roger, let me know when Ice gets here."

"Will do."

"Let's go guys," I said.

We headed into the bay. As soon as we stepped off the steps, alarm bells started going off in my head. They were too late, because the door slammed shut and the lights went out.

The bay was dark, except for the light spilling out of the gaping hole in the middle of the floor. *"Looks like a mouth ready to swallow you up huh Bri." "Well you told him to come on and here's what you get dumb ass."*

We had our flashlights on and were panning around the bay, when we heard the familiar ring. It was coming from the hole.

I said aloud, maybe too loud, "Not this time mother fucker. You may have trapped us in here, but there is no fucking way were going in that hole."

"Amen to that" was Ken's response.

Then the radio, the four of the echoed in

the bay,

"Chief, this is Ice, where the hell are you."

I responded quickly, "In the bay, use rear access if you can."

"Copy, on my way."

Within a minute the drive through overhead came up and the lights came back on. Ice was standing there puzzled.

"Wasn't even locked." Then, as if he just remembered, "any sign of Shawn?"

I shook my head. "Maybe over there," I motioned toward the hole, "but I don't think so."

Ice cupped his hands and yelled "SHAWN!" but got no answer.

We all tried several times, without any luck. I hated to think Shawn might be in the hole. Since he didn't answer us and was no where else we could find, I had to assume he was.

We carefully made our way to the hole. Ice and I went in, while the others held the doors. It was hot as hell in there, but no sign of Shawn.

We went back up, closed the doors and walked to the loading deck. Standing in the doorway I asked Ice.

"He take the truck?"

He nodded. "Near as I can tell he did, his car was already here."

"What now chief," Hank asked.

"Back to the bus and regroup," I answered.

As soon as the last of us stepped out of the bay, the door went down with a slam, barely missing Ken. I checked, this time it was locked. We'd lost round one.

As we were walking back to the bus, my cell

rang. It was Tom.

"I got some info for you, it ain't much."

."Give me what you got."

"Englewood Foundation, opened under a government grant, guess which department."

"Defense," I answered.

"Right," he came back. "They broke ground Mid-August 1939 on the Tulsa Facility. It went operational a year later. Director of Operations listed as Jacob Harris PHD."

"Place closed "Under Suspicious Circumstances," August 21, 1942. That's all I got so far. I'm getting a bit more and I'll bring it to the bus. Should be another hour or so."

"Thanks Tom, good work, by the way keep an eye out for Shawn ok."

"OK, anything I should know?"

"I'll fill you in when you get here."

I hung up and relayed to the guys what Tom had told me. Just before we could talk about it, my cell rang again. Caller ID said it was Shay.

I answered; figuring this was a call to check on us.

"Chief don't ask no questions just get here and bring Ice. Shawn's out on the lawn just staring at the house, and Brian, he's got a gun."

"On the way. Bruiser stay here with dispatch, the rest of you come with me."

"Where we going?" Ice asked.

"My place."

I filled them, in while proving what my Ramcharger would do. As we turned the corner onto my street we all saw the white truck.

"How the fuck did that get past us?" I yelled.

"It couldn't have," Ken's answered, "not as

far as I know. It would have had to drive right
by the bus."

We pulled out front. Shawn was still there.
He had a gun in his hand, but it was down to his
side. Ice pleaded his case.

"Let me handle this chief, he's my
brother."

"It's all yours for now Ice."

Ice walked slowly towards Shawn, talking
low and soft. Shawn relaxed his grip on the gun
and it slid to the ground, followed by Shawn, out
cold.

Shay came out of the house holstering her
gun. I have no doubt, if he had made the wrong
move, he would have been dead.

My cell rang again. This time the caller ID
showed only a number; 555-812-1942. I looked at
my watch, it was just after five, I answered it.
It was the angry voice.

"What do you think I could have made him do Bri? You still think the little bitch is safe? I told you not to fuck with me Bri."

I hung up and took Ice to the side. "Man I know he's your brother, but we have got to put him someplace safe for now."

He looked down then back at me. "Your right chief and I know it, but it ain't easy. He's all I got left man."

I nodded. "I know, that's why we gotta get him someplace safe."

I made a call and pulled in some favors. Within an hour Shawn was in a safe hospital, medicated and supervised the next morning he would be on a plane, to a quiet place, on the bay, in Maryland.

I called Bruiser and he told me things were quiet. He and his girl were gonna stay there, they would call if anything changed. I could see there was nothing more we were gonna do that

146

night and sent everyone home.

Ice stayed at my place that night. Before we turned in he took me aside.

"That *thing* fucked with my brother Chief, now we gotta finish it."

"I couldn't agree more."

I didn't know what to tell him. I had no words that would ease the pain he had to be in.

"I promise you Ice, we will finish it"

I left him with that went to my room. I got to sleep in my own bed that night. It was still a little cold, but at least she was there.

August 6

Bailey woke me the next morning. She was still upset, but at least she was talking to me.

"Shay and I are going to take care of the new offices today. They are in different buildings. So, for now anyway, Operations and administration will be about two miles apart. We can lease them both through the same agent so, it will be easier."

"How soon can we move in?"

"Lady said we can have the keys on the 15th, so we should have everything up and running by the 18th."

"Twelve more days," I sighed, "guess that'll work."

She changed the subject. "Bri, I wish you would reconsider and let us be a part of this."

"Bailey, think about it." "I have to be focused when I'm dealing with whatever the hell that is in there, if you were there, I would be worried about keeping you safe." "That's a distraction none of us need."

She stood up quick. "A distraction!" Her teeth were clenched and her hands were balled in fists. "Is that all I am to you? A distraction? Screw you Brian, you chauvinistic ass. I have a meeting to get too, BOSS. Go chase your ghosts."

Her and Shay left without another word. I looked across the table at Hank.

"That's not what I meant." He just shrugged.

I thought about all the times that I had mishandled similar conversations with Carol, my ex. *"You're on a roll Bri. You are on a roll."*

The seven of us met at nine, in the back of the bus. It was time to discuss a different strategy.

"Tom, what were you able to find out?"

He looked down at his noted, cleared his throat and began. "Well in the few days after this facility closed, City, County and State police got several missing persons reports. Within a week, an order came down that all inquiries about Englewood Foundation, would be referred to a special office in the Federal Building."

"By the end of August Englewood Foundation closed all of their facilities and ceased to exist. That's all the information I could get Chief. I tried to dig for the MP reports, but they are long gone."

"Well," I said after a minute, "the MP reports might explain why it looked like they went to lunch."

Ken shook his head. "No, no way, this place

had to employ 150 or so people. I don't think the Government could make that many people disappear at once today, much less fifty years ago."

"Gentlemen," I said, "something happened to those people and the answer has got to be in that building somewhere. I think we need to find it."

They all expressed their agreement, in one way or another.

"First step we tackle those upstairs offices."

Ken added, "this time we ignore his distractions." I cringed at the word, but agreed.

The pool was exactly the way that we had left it and the door to the bay was still locked. We went upstairs and I unlocked the first office, which wasn't and office at all, not exactly.

This room had been set up as a laboratory. We spread out and started going through cabinets and drawers.

"Grab anything that looks interesting," I said. "We'll take it back to the bus and digest it there."

Truth was, I didn't want to spend more time in there than I had to. We were stuffing files into plastic trash bags we had brought, when the phone down the hall started ringing. *"Ignore the distractions."* I thought and let it ring. I guess our host was unhappy with our decision, because the phone stopped ringing and the heavy wooden door slammed shut.

Bruiser went to it but it was locked.

"Leave it," I told him. "Let's finish here first."

We quickly took all of the files, no longer caring if they looked interesting. Now, he might be able to close doors, which told me reason no longer mattered. The laws of physics however still applied. The wooden door, was no match for Hank and Gunner's bulk.

As we started down the stairs, I looked back. "Might take you some time to fix that one Buddy."

The files we had retrieved gave us some information, but not much. There were a lot of pages of test results on lab animals. We had even found a key code that crossed drug numbers to chemical descriptions. Nothing, anywhere that described A-21 or even mentioned it.

I was getting discouraged when the dispatcher called out. "Mr. Kelly, there is a Jacob Harris on line one for you."

I was about to put him on speaker, when I had another thought.

I went to the dispatcher station and scrolled back the caller ID. The number was there 555-821-1942. Then my eyes caught the top of the systems printout and something clicked.

The top of the page read 08-06-1992. *"That ain't a fuckin number Bri, that's a fuckin date."*

At least I had something.

I went back to the back and hit the speakerphone.

"You're not Jacob either buddy, so what do you want now?"

"Now Bri," It was the nice and calm voice this time, "be nice, I let you have the files didn't I? Pardon my being rude, hello to the rest of you too." He knew we were all listening. "Now breaking the door, that hurt Bri. You want to know what that felt like Bri?"

"Like I give a fuck," I answered.

"Well let me show you." I felt a pain in my arm, but only for a moment. "It didn't hurt long Bri. Now listen, what you have isn't important, not to me anyway. It belongs here Bri, it's part of me, so I trust you will put it back, when you are done."

"Part of you?"

The voice laughed, "nice try Bri. "It's part of this place, and it belongs to me. You have taken so much from me already Bri." "Most of it I can never get back."

"Why don't you tell me about August 21, 1942?" I asked."

He laughed again, "figured it out finally genius?" "It doesn't matter."

I pushed him, "Tell me, what does matter?"

The voice changed "listen you arrogant prick, I'll tell you what I choose to tell you. We sat here, unmolested for fifty years. You had to come along and fuck that up. You may think you are getting answers, but they won't help you."

This time I laughed, "if they won't help, why are you getting scared?"

"This fucking conversation is over." The line went dead.

We sat and stared at the phone for awhile.

Gunner spoke first.

"That is one seriously disturbed mother fucker."

"Sure is," I added, "and we are making him nervous."

Ken asked, "what's this shit about August 21, 1942?"

"I think that's the key. We stop looking for A-21. It's just another code. Start looking for anything that refers to August 21st."

We read until about 14:30 when Bailey and Shay showed up with lunch for everyone. I guess I'd lost that argument. No point in pushing my luck.

While we ate we talked about what we had been reading. Ken and Hank had both been reading some stuff about mind control drugs.

"They tested this shit on rats and made them do things." Hank said.

Ken added, "then they moved to human subjects." "They could make them do serious stuff. Made one guy walk straight in front of a moving truck. Report said he lived."

"One thing in common, none of them remembered anything. They even started using this shit on their research assistants. Even the people in their typing pool." One of these files talks about noting but unusual sexual activities, they made those innocent girls do some unbelievable shit. I couldn't read anymore."

"Me either," Hank confirmed.

I had been reading the section on performance enhancement drugs. Not much there, a lot of stuff about super strength and a few references to increasing sexual duration.

Bruiser and Gunner had been reading about sensory depravation experiments and had nothing of interest to add.

Tom, however, had hit pay dirt at least he

found the opening.

"Chief a lot of those files make a reference to something that was supposed to take place on August 21st." They were waiting on something from Dallas."

"Tom, what were you reading about?"

"Well, they mostly talk about effects of electromagnetic impulses on the test subjects. Something about how certain phase induction makes them shimmer."

"OK," I said, "keep those files separate. The rest of them, fuck it, just dump them in the pool. If he wants to put them away, more power to him. Tomorrow, we check the other offices. This time I want personnel files."

I looked at Bailey and Shay. "I guess you're going to join us tomorrow." I gave in.

We put the files in the box and I locked the door. Bruiser and his girl had taken up permanent residence in the bus. The rest of us went home.

Hank, Shay and Bailey were still at my place. Ken had sent his family to his wife's mothers. Ice was going to stay with him. I knew I'd get a call that night. I wasn't disappointed.

August 7

The call from Bruiser came at 00:45. "Chief, just thought you should know there's some weird shit going on over there."

"What kind of shit Bruiser?"

"Well mostly banging, all the lights are on, but the weird part is that truck showed up just before everything started. Just pulled right up to the door. Saw it with my own eyes. Nobody got out, but all the other shit started right away. It's still there too, nobody in the cab, just idling away like gas is still a nickel a gallon."

"Want me to come down?"

"Nope, just thought you should know. Didn't nobody go in there, cause I watched. I called Ken's place, he and Ice were there watching the tube. As far as they knew, the truck was at your place."

"I thought so too. Let me know if anything changes. We'll check it out in the morning."

"Sure chief, I won't call unless it gets crazy around here."

I hung up the phone and Bailey reached across

the bed.

"Maybe it's time to let it go Bri."

"I can't, not yet. Not until I've helped Shawn."

At least that she could understand. It was true, I had to do that, but it was only part of it. I lay back down and she cuddled up next to me for the first time in what seemed like ages.

We had a quick breakfast the next morning and drove together to the bus. I had one piece of business to take care of before we made our daily trip to hell. I called my friend at this little retreat on the Chesapeake Bay. Once I got him, I put him on the speaker.

"So, how's your newest guest?" I asked.

"Young Mr. Poole seems to be fine." "He shows no signs that anything is wrong. He has moments, when he gets pissed at being here, but who wouldn't. My only concern is that he has reported having very little memory of the last few days, before he got here. Mostly, I keep him medicated like you asked."

Ice chimed in. "Doug, can you give him a message for me?"

"I'd be more than happy to Stephen. In fact he has one for you. He said to tell you he was sorry he let you down and he loves you."

Ice almost lost it. "That's the same message I wanted to give him."

"I'll take care of him Stephen, don't worry. Is there anything else Brian?"

"No, thanks Doug, I owe you."

"No Brian, you don't, this doesn't even make us even."

We gathered our gear and more bags and headed to the task at hand. The files we had left in the bay, were gone. The door we had broken the day before was as good as new.

I opened the door to the next office, but before we could go in, it slammed shut in our faces. I tried to open it again, but it was locked and my key wouldn't work. I motioned to Hank and Gunner.

"Take it off the fucking hinges."

Before they could comply with my wishes, the Black phone in my office started ringing.

"FUCK," I yelled.

I turned and went to my office. I picked the phone off the desk, pulled out my K-bar and cut the cord. Did I really expect that to work? It didn't. I threw the damn thing, out the door, into the hall. The receiver was off, but it continued to ring. Exasperated I pulled my 9mm, six rounds later the bastard quit ringing.

I rejoined the others and nodded to Hank. The three of us hit the door at the same time. It gave, flying in several directions. When I opened the first file drawer, I realized this was the personnel office.

"Take every file," I said. "Check the desks too, and do it fast."

With nine of us working it didn't take very long. We went back downstairs; the door to the pool was open, inviting us in for a look. I kicked it closed.

"Not this time asshole." It opened again anyway. I shook my head, "persistent little shit aren't you? Let's get out of here."

It wasn't as easy as it sounded. The door wouldn't open. It was a much stronger door than the ones upstairs and it opened inward.

My K-bar came in handy again. I removed the hinge pins and pried the door open that way. It took all our efforts, but we got out. We were less than ten feet away and the door was already back in place.

As we entered the bus Mandy informed me "Your guys calling again, he's on line one."

"Well, let's hear what he has to say."

I hit the speaker button. It was the mean voice this time, from the start.

"Now Bri, that wasn't nice at all. Why do you insist on fucking with things that don't belong to you?"

"Listen asshole," I said losing my temper, "I own that building and therefore legally it all belongs to me."

"Legality don't have a fucking thing to do with this Bri. Jacob used to worry about the law too, didn't do him any good either. We are beyond the law here. It simply doesn't fucking apply to us. But, let's stick to the fucking point Bri. I don't want you looking in those files. They won't help you and just might hurt innocent people."

"From what I read shit head, not very many of those people were innocent. Not after you psychos got done with them."

The voice was a little calmer now. "Well yes, we did do some interesting things, didn't we, but I digress again. Bri, I want you to take those files back now. Those people have families, leave them alone."

"They have families and that's why I can't leave them alone. They deserve to know what happened, They deserve the truth. My arm started to hurt and the pain was getting worse.

"Don't make me punish you again Bri. I may have to start on the pretty young thing Bailey over there. I have a connection with her to Bri, and more than just her arm. It would be interesting to see her go from innocent virgin to sadistic slut, don't you think Bri?"

I thought about it for a minute, "You can't," I said calmly, "or you already would have."

"Don't fucking push me Brian." And the line went dead.

I looked at Bailey, she was terrified, so was I. I hoped he was bluffing.

There were exactly two hundred and fifty-seven files on employees, volunteers and test subjects. Everything went up to, or just before, August 21, 1942. The file on Jacob Harris was missing.

The one file I was most interested in was for a Supervising Test Engineer, named Stewart Kensington. His records showed he had started at the Philadelphia facility, transferred first to Dallas, then to Tulsa on July 16th 1942. I crossed checked all the files we had

kept. His signature was on all of them.
Bailey, Shay and Tom were making a list of the
names.

"After you get that done, lets get those files
back to the pool."

I went outside for a smoke and some fresh air.
Hank followed.

"Chief, I think you should know, Bailey's
taking anti-depressants, has since her mom
died. That might have something to do with
what sets her apart from you and Shawn."

"Probably has a lot to do with it, That, and
the fact that she's strong. Shawn wasn't"

We got the files back in the pool without
incident. I had a feeling we had gotten all
the answers from upstairs we were going to get
for now. What we needed now was in the bay
somewhere, probably in the hole. I knew we
needed to get those files back. I had a
feeling that wasn't going to be easy.

"Let's call it a day. Ice, I need you to see
if you can round us up a torch, preferably a
pack type. I have a feeling we are going to
need it."

Bailey hadn't said much, so after dinner I
took her into the den.

"Bri, can he really control me like he did
Shawn?" She was shaking, so I held her.

"No, at least I don't think so, but you have
to keep taking your pills. Don't even miss
one."

"How, how did you know?" she looked
embarrassed.

"Hank told me, don't say anything to him, "
I'm glad he did."

"How did he know about the other thing, about
me being a, well you know."

"Because you're innocent, that's something
Shawn and I are not. That's another reason he
can't touch you."

I wanted her to believe that last part, more
than anything I wanted it to be true.

August 8

Monday presented us with new problems. Our
sales force needed a place to work. They had
calls to make and contracts to write. I
couldn't expect them to keep working out of
their houses and without their computers.
Renting four rooms at the Best Western would
solve part of that problem. We could forward
the phones there.

The next part was more difficult. They need
the stuff from their offices, and for that we
had to let them into the building. This
included the installation department. What
they needed was in the bay. I gathered the
troops in the back of the bus.

"Ok, we need to get the sales people moved out
first." That's the easy part. If all of us
work on it, it shouldn't take long. Ice, while
we're doing that, you get the install guys
together. Have each of them make a list of the
shit they need out of the bay. Make sure they
get enough to last them awhile. I don't want
to have to do this again soon. Did you get
that torch?"

"Sure did chief, it's in my truck."

"Good I want it handy while we're in the bay.

Let's get the sales guys done."

If someone who didn't know what was going on saw us, they would of thought we looked silly. I posted a guard, armed uniformed patrol, at each door.

"Hold those damn things open."

I led everyone upstairs single file. When I got to the top, I noticed the door we had busted in the day before. It was back in place, but it wasn't perfect. I could still see cracks where the door had broken. There were noticeable pieces missing.

I let it go for the moment. We needed to get this done.

"Grab what you need. We'll help carry."

In less than twenty minuets we had the sales offices empty. Bailey, you and Shay, take these guys up to the hotel. Get them settled in, and then get the hell back here. The hard parts next."

I leaned against Bailey's mustang and lit a smoke. Hank joined me.

"You see that fuckin door chief?"

"Yeah, kinda shity workmanship huh?"

"You think its losing control?"

"Could be Hank, could also be what he wants us to think."

"Tough call."

"I ain't ready to make it." Tom was on his cell, shaking his head and walking my way.

"Another problem?"

"You remember those extra patrol car you asked for?"

"Ah shit."

"They took our bid. They are loading them on the trucks as we speak. I tried to get them to hold off, but policy says they have to move them."

"How many?"

"Sixteen."

"Oh hell, how much?" "Eighty-six grand, including fees and transport."

"Thanks Tom, perfect fuckin timing."

"Just doing my job chief."

"I know."

"Good thing is all we have to do is slap a sticker on them and they are ready to go."

"What'd you get?"

"Nine Crown Vic's and seven Caprice Classics. All 1990 models and they're police resale so the tags are good." "Guess we can all drive one, keep the lot clear."

"Sure thing chief." He walked away looking less than happy.

"Hey Tom, good work, just a little faster than I expected."

Hank slapped me on the shoulder, on his way to the bus. "Not a nice recovery chief." I walked around back to find Ice.

"Got your list together?"

"Yep, even grouped things together to save time."

"Good, go to the bus and get everyone. Let's get this going."

"Ain't you gonna wait for Shay and Bailey?"
"Ice, man, I'd just rather they weren't here is all."

"Got'cha chief. I'll get the others."

"Better get a grip Bri, you need these people." *"What the fuck are you thinking man, these people are your friends."*

Ice came back with the others as six Dakotas and two half tons backed up to the loading dock.

"Figured I'd get them in close and same some time."

"Good thinking Ken. I want every door opened. No less than four people in the building at any time and no less than two on the outside. If anything is going to happen today, it's going to be here. One final rule, stay the hell away from the hole."

 As soon as all the doors were open, Ken, Bruiser, Hank and I stepped into the bay accompanied by eight installers. We had no sooner got in when the doors started back down. Gunner got under one and tried to hold it open. Hank and Bruiser tried to help. The installers took advantage and hurried out. They lost their grip on the door. It was just Ken and me in the bay.

The good thing was the light stayed on. "I yelled through the door.

"Ice cut a hole in this mother fucker, a big one."

"Did you figure on this?"

"Somethin like it anyway."

"What happens now?"

"We wait until Ice gets that hole cut. After that, we do what we came here for."

"Fair enough." I lit a smoke.

"Chief you ever think of just goin fishin?"

"Doin what?"

"Goin fishin, just saying fuck it all and hittin Keystone or Grand for a few weeks." Enjoying your retirement."

"Ken, where in the hell did that come from?"

"That'd be what I'm thinkin right about now."

"What made you think of that?"

"Cause I'd rather be doin that, instead of bein here with you right now. Nothin personal understand."

"Yeah Ken, ok."

The torch had just started cutting through the door. The doors to the hole flew open with a bang. We both jumped.

"Now what the fuck?"

"Usually, when that happens the lights go next." We pulled our flashlights just in case. It was getting cold fast.

"Help me Bri."

It came from the hole; there was no mistaking the voice. I started forward. Ken pulled me back.

"She ain't in there, you saw her leave. It's a

fuckin trap."

"I just have to be sure."

"You just gotta be staying right the fuck here. Wait until we get some help."

I looked at the door. Nowhere near close enough.

"Just gonna have a look."

"You even act like you gonna go in there, I'll shoot you. I ain't playin chief. I'll take out your other knee if I have to."

"Bri, help me please."

It sounded like she was crying now. I walked faster. I crept to the front edge of the hole. I couldn't see very far.

"BAILEY!"

"God Bri, help me please I can't get out."

"Where's Shay Bailey?"

"I...I'm not sure she...Bri come get me out of this cage, *please*."

I got on my knees and looked into the hole. I caught the movement out of the corner of my eye. I rolled out of the way real quick. I felt the wind, as the door slammed shut, missing me by less than an inch.

"Goddamnit chief! You about lost your fuckin head. I told you she ain't in there and you know it. Come on now, back over by the door. They're almost through."

"Close one, huh Ken?"

"Man, this mother fucker tried to kill you."

I grabbed my cell as we walked back to the

door. I had no signal.

"Hank, my cells dead, try to call Shay and Bailey."

"My cells dead to chief. I'm gonna go use a phone in the bus."

"Make it quick man."

Ice was almost three-quarters of the way through with a four by six hole. The phone in the hole started ringing.

"Don't you even think about it chief. Ya hear that mother fucker, we don't want to talk to your ass."

I chose my next words carefully and spoke to the walls. "Stewart, or do you prefer Mr. Kensington?" The ringing stopped. "Your taking over this place didn't go like you planned, did it Stewart? I read your file Stewie."

"Man, you trying to piss it off or what?"

"Somehow, one of your little projects went fucking haywire. Fucked up your whole day, didn't it? Now you're stuck here and pissed off. What you sow, so shall you reap, dumb ass."

"Look out! Coming in."

A big piece of the door fell into the bay. The doors all started going up. Ice clapped me on the back.

"That was one hell of a speech."

"Yeah, let's get this done. Tom, give me a hand. While we're here, might as well get the decals for the cars."

"Sure, they're unloading them now.

We got all of the equipment we needed without incident.

Hank came back and told me Shay and Bailey were fine. They were on their way back. They made it about the time we left the loading dock. We just left the door up.

Way I figured it. Anyone crazy enough to try and steal anything from the bay, got what they deserved.

It was getting late, but we all went with Tom to check our new vehicle inventory. It looked like a police sub-station out front. They were all in decent shape. I figured they averaged about seven grand each. We didn't do too badly.

We spent the next hour enjoying the mundane task of putting the decals on each one. We were joking around, horse-playing and generally having a good time. We each picked one to be our company car for now.

I personally thought the Crown Vic's looked a bit more, bad ass, than the Caprice. Others didn't share my opinion. That night there were three of them at my house. Bailey had driven her Mustang back to her apartment and I picked her up there. She would get her caprice tomorrow. As much stuff as she put in the back seat, it would have led anyone to believe she was moving in. Don't think, for one second, I minded at all.

I held her real close that night and fell asleep wondering what I would have done if she had been in the hole.

August 9

I'd hardly slept. The last few days kept
playing in my mind, which I felt like I was
losing. I couldn't help but think I was
missing something important. Whatever happened
in that building, 50 years ago, had caused a
lot of people to vanish.

Somehow, this Kensington guy had been linked
with this building; he'd become part of it. I
thought about that. Hell, if I'd been stuck
in the same place for fifty years, I'd be
pissed too. No chance of escape, was a hell of
a price to pay for near immortality. Maybe the
truth would set him free. Maybe, that's what
he was afraid of.

When I got to the bus that morning, I had no
intention of going in the building that day. I
had no reason to. I figured today, I would get
caught up on some work. I had a stack of stuff
that needed my attention.

In spite of everything else our business was
growing. We were desperately going to need
more patrol people. I figured that could wait
until we got moved. Most of the others had
work of their own to get done.

Bailey and Shay were off meeting with the

Leasing Agent. Ice and Ken were with the sales guys. Tom was downtown doing research on the list we had made of "former employees." Hank was on patrol doing initial evaluations and getting a feel for things. Gunner had the day off.

Bruiser, as usual, was in the bus. I was compelled; however, to check a few things out before I tackled the paperwork.

I walked around back to the loading dock. I expected to find the doors still open. They were closed. The hole we'd cut was fixed, but, like the door upstairs, it wasn't perfect. You could see the outline. There were holes here and there. It was like someone had patched it. *"He's getting tired."*

I looked through the windows of the two garages. My heart skipped a beat when I saw the Ambulance missing. I remembered it, as well as, the Caddy had been sent away and were being equipped as patrol units. The white truck was back in garage two. Englewood Foundation, clearly showing through the cover paint.

I went to the bus, exchanged pleasantries with Bruiser and Mandy and sat down to work. Tom's call surprised me.

"I've got a nice little piece of information I thought you might need to know. Stewart Kensington didn't vanish with everyone else on August 21st. He wasn't even there. Came back from Philly the next day."

"Where the hell did you get all this?" "From his wife. She's alive and well in Dallas. She said he came back on the 22nd, went to work as usual and came home an hour later, scared as hell. She told me he made a couple of calls and wouldn't leave the house after that."

"Chief, she woke up on the morning of August 26th and he was gone. She filed a missing persons and a couple of days later got a visit. Bunch of 'Government Types.' They gave her a shit load of money and warned her to keep quiet."

"I guess my phone call ended that. Boss she seemed real eager to tell me all she knew."

"She say anything about what he was workin on?"

"I don't think he told her about it." "She said he spent a lot of time flying between here, Dallas and Philly. Only thing he told her after he got back was something about a fire.

"He may have been coverin something else with that, good work Tom"

"I'll keep looking chief, later."

It made no sense. I was sure A-21 stood for an experiment set to take place on August 21st. I knew A-21 was Kensington's project. Why would he be gone that day? Would they do it without him there? What's all this shit about a fire? If that's not Kensington, then just who the hell is it? *Too many questions, not near enough answers."*

My paperwork forgotten, I put through a call to my old friend Ed. Watkins.

Ed was a former FBI field agent I'd worked with in the past. His hard work, dedication and shear genius landed him a job in the basements of Quantico. It took a while, but I finally got him.

"Hi Ed, Brian Kelly."

"My God Kelly, I haven't heard from you in ages. To be honest, I didn't ever expect to. I heard about that thing in Iraq. I'm Sorry to hear it. How are things with you now Brian?"

"Mostly good Ed. I have my own business now, just tryin to start over."

"Excellent. So, I guess you started that Security consulting thing after all. But, I know you didn't call me just to catch up. Is there something I can help you with?"

"I think you can Ed. My business is in a building that used to be part of The Englewood Foundation."

"Hold on just a second Brian. Did you say Englewood?"

"Yeah, why?"

"I don't think we want to talk about this Brian."

"What the hell does that mean Ed."

"Brian, let me tell you this. Here we have keywords. When we hear or see one of those keywords, a red flag goes up. For as long as I can remember, Englewood has been one of those keywords. It's funny, because lately I have been hearing it a lot."

"I guess you guys heard from the DOD guys then."

"Yes, but how did you know that?"

"They were here, taking stuff out not long ago Ed. I need to know as much as I can, about this place in general, and Stewart Kensington specifically."

"My God Brian, don't ever say that name to me again. I have the hit sheet on that one now. Seems like you, or someone, has been doing some digging. Brian I like you and I owe you my life. So let me do you a favor. Drop this. Do it now. Cut your losses and walk away."

"Damn it Ed, I can't cut my losses. My losses include a kid I had to send up to Doug's bird farm. I owe it to that kid, and his brother, to get some answers."

"Brian, I am going to forget we had this conversation. I can only forget it, if you let me. Eventually, someone is going to put the pieces together, they may have already, then they might start asking you questions Brian. I cannot be caught in the middle of that."

"That, may not be a good idea Ed. You know me, what you may not know is, I have a big part of my team with me. Think about that, before you unleash the hounds. Give my best to your wife and kid Ed."

I slammed the phone down. I hadn't realized that Bailey and Shay had come in while I was on the phone.

"Looks like all our diggin has ruffled some feathers down at the Hoover Building."

"How much trouble are we in Bri?"

"None yet, that I know about."

"May come soon enough."

"How about some lunch ladies?"

The phone on the table rang, just as we were leaving. This phone didn't have a direct dial number. I picked it up.

"Kelly Security."

"Good Afternoon Bri,"

The far away voice caught me off guard and I pushed the speaker button.

"It appears we have some catching up to do."

"I'm tried of this crap. You have nothin to say, I care to hear."

"Oh, I think you're wrong Bri. I think you would be very interested in hearing what I have to say."

"Well, impress me then."

"Please don't be a smartass Brian. I am far to weary at this point to put up with your insolence."

"Could you get to the point, I have a lunch date."

"How interesting, I hope your lovely associate remembered to take her medication today." One look at her told me she hadn't.

"Fuck"

"See Bri, now you have to listen."

"Ok, you have my attention."

"Good, no more of your mouth either."

"For now."

"Fair enough. From here on I call the shots. Unless, you want to send your bitch off to be with the kid." Bailey's hands were shaking, but she was fine.

"I don't think you have that power over her."

"Shall we find out Brian?"

"No, what the hell do you want."

"I want you, Brian. You have caused me a lot of pain. I need to repay you. I want you to come to me alone."

"Bri, NO! There is no way that is going to happen." "You still don't have me."

The voice change was immediate. "Shut the fuck up slut."

Bailey bent double in pain. He may not be able to control her, but he could hurt her.

"You leave her alone motherfucker. Shay get her out of here." Bailey wouldn't be moved.

"You want me? You got it, but not the way you think. I'll come for you not to you. Starting now!"

I slid the buses side window open, pulled my gun and emptied the clip into the side of the building. We could hear the static grow with each shot. By the time the gun stopped firing, the line was dead.

"Shay, take Bailey home. Take your pills and anything you can think of Bailey."

"Bri, I'm sorry I forgot. I do that, now and then."

I put my arms around her. "It's not your fault."

"Don't go in there alone."

Tim Hancock

"I won't, I promise. Shay, don't let her out of your sight, until we're sure she'll be ok."

"Have no fear honey. I'll handcuff her young ass if I have to. She'll be fine chief, once she gets drugged up that is."

She led Bailey to her car.

"Bruiser, round up the troops." I sat in the back of the bus, waiting.

Within an hour everyone but Gunner and the girls were with me in the back of the bus. I told them everything beginning with Tom's call and ending with shots fired. After I finished, there was a prolonged silence. Hank was the first to speak.

"So ol Ed's finally became another agency tool. How easy we forget."

Tom asked, "what's the story?" "Short version is Chief here saved Ed's balls at a landing strip, down in Columbia. I mean really saved his balls, no figure of speech there. Then, about six months later, we rescued his wife and young daughter, from that same group of crazies. Fed's really fucked that one up."

"Were they going to cut his balls off?"

Ken laughed. Everyone here knew the story but Tom.

Hank continued. "Fifteen year old had them fuckers in one hand and a big ass machete in the other. Chief here takes the kid out, with a three round burst, from about two hundred yards. Ol Ed pissed then and there, funny as hell.

"So then they grabbed his family?"

182

"Yeah, a revenge thing. That kid was some big shit's heir apparent. They had no idea who chief here was, so they grabbed the two ladies to find out. They got to meet the chief. But we're tellin the story, not them."

"Let's move on guys, OK."

"What you got in mind chief?"

"I want to look in those two offices. I don't think we got a lot of time. The way I figure it, the FBI, or someone like them will be here in a few days. Ice, you bring that pack torch. Everybody get cocked, locked and ready to rock."

My key wouldn't unlock the outside door, but the 12 gage did. We went upstairs and straight to the first office we wanted. I couldn't unlock it either.

"Give me that gut buster again." The door opened on it's own. "Ice, that door closes, fire up that torch and burn it down." It didn't close.

There wasn't much of anything in that office, just the weird feeling. What few files and notes were there, we took. We moved quickly to the next office. The door was already open. Sometimes violence *does* pay.

Inside the office felt like December. This was the only office in the place with a safe and a locked file cabinet. They were 1940's crap, so the torch made short work of both.

We grabbed the files from the cabinet but the good stuff was in the safe. Lots of files labeled A-21. Pay dirt.

We made our way downstairs, but our host
wasn't done. As we got into the bay a desk
came sliding fast. We dodged it easily, but it
blocked the door. The other desks in the pool
moved to aid their comrade. File cabinet
division, had been assigned to block the new
fire exit and were already in position.

Bruiser, said, half laughing "Motherfucker,
they got us surrounded chief."

I fired a shotgun round into the floor.

"Easy way, or hard way, motherfucker?" The
door to the bay opened. "Hard way. Ice!"

He lit the torch. The makeshift sentries moved
in on us. Instead of attacking a desk, Ice put
the torch to the closest wall. The troops
stood down and let us through. Once outside
Hank turned to me.

"I guess we hurt it."

"I think *that's* where our problem started
Hank. We hurt HIM first.

We stashed the files in my makeshift office,
in the back of the bus. I figured I would look
at them tomorrow. I wanted to get home and
check on Bailey. It would be a few days before
I would get back to them files. I'd know most
of it by then anyway.

When Hank and I got home, we found the girls
relaxing out by the pool. If nothing else, it
was a pleasant sight. I took Baileys hand.

"How's it goin?"

"Had some pain for awhile, got better the
farther away we got. It quit all together
after awhile."

"After a Valium, you mean. I gave her one of those and her regular stuff too. "Didn't figure it'd hurt anything. Seemed to help her relax, if nothin else."

"What did you find out Bri?"

"Well, we can hurt him. If we can hurt him, we can control him."

"Well why don't you guys get changed." "We have some beer on ice and steak on fire. Still plenty of time to enjoy the water."

I looked at her, standing there, in a skimpy, pink string bikini.

"Them steaks ain't the only thing on fire."

We had a great time the rest of the night. Once again, we were able to separate ourselves, from the evil less than five miles away. I slept good, that night. My dreams filled with visions, of a pink string bikini.

Tim Hancock

August 10

As Bailey and I pulled into the lot the next morning, those pleasant visions departed. Well not completely but they were put on hold.

There were two marked county units, two unmarked units and a new black Crown Victoria that could only belong to the Feds. Even the two guys leaning on it and smoking were typical Bureau issue. They wore the same crumpled brown suites and sunglasses.

The shorter of the two seemed to be in charge, and probably told everyone about it. They started towards us, before we got parked.

"Brian Kelly." The way he said it was more statement than question. "My name is Parker and this here's Special Agent Eastman. We are from the FBI."

The last part was for those who may be listening, but were far to stupid to notice the obvious. I sat on the fender of my own Crown Vic.

"Go ahead Bailey, I'll catch up."

Tall goon "Eastman," grabbed Baileys arm.

"Hold on Miss. Krikwood, we want to talk to you too."

186

I gave him a cold stare and spoke softly. "Young man, you ever put a hand on her again, the Bureau's gonna be buying you a new one at Lowes."

He let her go. I nodded to her and she continued toward the bus. Little goon moved in front of me, in a desperate attempt to be the center of attention.

"Brian, why don't we go inside and talk."

Little fool, not only called me Brian, like we were friends, but he was motioning towards the building.

"That's not likely to happen."

"Why is that Brian?" "Mr. Kelly."

My voice stayed soft and even. I was kind of trying a Clint Eastwood thing.

"How's that?"

"Mr. Kelly."

"What do you mean, Mr. Kelly." He was thick headed too.

"Your Mr. Parker, I'm Mr. Kelly. Until we are drinking beers and shootin darts at Palmroy's on the Circle, that's the way it stays."

"I see, but that is Special Agent Parker, not Mister."

"Fine Parker. Say, what are you, Assistant Resident Agent or something?"

Tall goon snickered, I gathered I was right.

"Why isn't that going to happen, MR. Kelly?"

"Give you three reasons Parker. First, I haven't seen a warrant. Second, I'd much rather talk to the Resident Agent in Charge. Finally, if I talk to anyone, it ain't gonna be in there."

"I can get a warrant."

"Get it."

"I can make you talk to me."

"Talk to my lawyer."

"I will get in that building."

"I have no doubt, and I know people that'll pay to see it."

"You are full of yourself aren't you Mr. Kelly?"

"Parker, you better take your little friends and leave."

"We are waiting on that warrant."

"Wait in the street."

"Mr. Kelly, I don't think you know who you are dealing with."

"You're wrong there Parker. I know full well. You, on the other hand are in the dark."

"Why don't you enlighten me then?"

"Sure, me, and that fella behind you, we're both former SEALs."

He looked back, Hank waved.

 "Now that alone tells me we have the two of you and the four Barneys outnumbered three-to-one. What you don't see. The other two SEALs and the rest of my highly trained team."

"You threatening me Mr. Kelly?"

"Nope just enlightenin you Parker. Now go,

before that changes."

"I'll be back Mr. Kelly."

"I'll be here, and Parker. Best if you brought your boss next time."

They left in short order. I figured they didn't go far and wouldn't be gone long. There was a lot of laughter, as we went in the bus.

One inside Tom let out a long whistle.

"I thought he was going to arrest you chief. He could have, for obstruction or something equally stupid."

"Sure, but that would have pissed his boss off. Bailey, get our lawyers on the phone, I think we're gonna need em."

We didn't have to wait long for the other shoe to drop.

They came back. This time they had a warrant to search the building for "Suspected items of interest to National Security." They had the RAC too. He was smarter than Parker was, but only barely.

"Mr. Kelly, I'm special agent Thomas." I left his offered hand empty. "I'm sure you already know Agents Parker and Eastman."

"We met."

"Mr. Kelly, if you attempt to interfere with us in any way, I will have you arrested for obstruction and charged with treason."

The last part stung, but I didn't let it show.

"Agent Thomas, you have my full cooperation."

"Good, Mr. Kelly, why don't the two of us go

inside and talk."

"I'll talk to you here or in my office in the command post. I'm just not up to going in there today."

He gave me a puzzled look. "I'll want to talk to your senior staff also."

"They're all in the bus. All but one, he's out of town."

"Right, that would be Shawn Poole. We know where he is, but can't get to him."

Parker spoke up. "Agent Thomas, would you please instruct MR. Kelly to unlock the doors for us."

He looked at me. I shrugged and handed him the keys.

"He can open it himself. I want it on record, all of my people were with you and nowhere near that building, while your guys were in there."

"Why is that, Mr. Kelly?"

"Cause that building has a mind of it's own Agent Thomas. I just want it on record. We had nothing to do with *anything* that happens."

"Such as?"

"God only knows Agent. Can I give you a word of advice Agent Thomas?"

"Sure, Mr. Kelly."

"Tell them not to all go in the hole in the receiving bay at the same time. They shouldn't answer the phone either."

I took Agent Thomas to my office in the bus

sitting him right on top of the files he was
looking for. The search team left one
uniformed officer at the door and the rest
went in.

I introduced Agent Thomas to my staff. The ten
of us crowded in the back of the Bus.

He took a thick file from his case, opened it
and started in with his questions.

"Mr. Kelly how did you acquire this property?"

"I traded my knee for it."

"What is your interest in the Englewood
Foundation?" "They were the previous tenants."

"Had some questions about the plumbing."

"Mr. Kelly, I thought you said you would
cooperate?"

"Sorry. There has been some weird stuff going
on. "It was causing some problems with my
staff. I wanted to know why."

"What do you know about Stewart Kensington?"

"A name I read in a file."

"What do you know about Samuel Brady?"

"Another name, in another file." I lied.

His questions continued in the same manner. I
was making mental notes, each time he gave me
more information. More names to look in to.
Some dates. Samuel Brady came up a lot.

About an hour into his interview, his cell
rang. He answered it, listened and got up and
looked out the window.

"Where are they now? Ok keep trying." He hung
up. \

"Problem Agent Thomas?"

"We can't reach my men. If you know something Mr. Kelly, I suggest you tell me now."

"I don't know enough Agent Thomas, that's the problem. There is something wrong with that building. Probably caused by some of the sick shit they did there. Near as I can tell, it had a lot to do with Kensington and Brady."

"Here's my deal Agent Thomas. We know a little about how to deal with this thing. So far, this has physically hurt no one, but that may change. If your guys are alive in there, we'll get them out. In exchange, you get your people off my back."

"I'm not sure I can."

"Thomas, my people are patriots. You'd be hard put to find a group more loyal to this country. While you think about that, we have work to do."

I had nine good people looking for six ignorant ones. I wasn't going to try this without Bailey and Shay. It's not like they'd have let me anyway. My thought was, this guy had been stuck as a part of this building for fifty years. These were government people. The government was responsible for him being where he was. Someone could actually get hurt this time.

We gathered the equipment I thought we would need. Two shotguns, the torch, and two fire axes, we liberated from the deputies' cars, as well as, our flashlights and side arms. I already had a plan of attack.

I figured they would have gone to the hole first, simply because my dumb ass had mentioned it. That's where I planned on going in. We took the white truck from the garage. Hank and I drove it through the over head door full speed.

I was right. A uniformed deputy and tall goon were by the closed doors to the hole.

"What happened?"

"They went in and the doors closed. They ain't locked, but we can't open them. We couldn't get out of here either. Mr. Kelly, I got three guys trapped down there."

"Three?"

"Yes sir, Agent Parker went up. Told me to take the other guys and check this out."

"Fuck me runnin! Ice; Cut that fuckin door off. In several pieces if needed. Hank, you and Bruiser come with me. You too Eastman."

The four of us ran to the door, leading to the pool.

"It's locked."

Hank pushed Eastman out of the way. "Yep, and this is an Axe."

The door split on the third hit. It was quiet in the pool. Yesterday's troops had gone back to their original duties, as office furniture. I sent Hank and Bruiser to the other stairs. Eastman and me went up the closer of the two.

"PARKER!" He didn't answer.

We started kicking in doors, using the shotgun twice to get them opened. I found Parker in the Old Lab. He was on the floor, under a heavy steel and glass equipment cabinet, which had somehow come unbolted from the floor. He was bleeding badly.

If it'd taken us much longer, he'd been dead." Hank and Bruiser carried him out and down. In the pool I treated the building to a counter of shotgun blasts. The door clicked open. We left Eastman with Parker and headed back to the bay.

When we got there, Ice was just getting the doors off the hole. While the shaken cops came out, he started cutting them in half. One of the cops had a small plastic bag, like the plastic off cigarettes in his hand.

"What's that?"

"Some of that dirt, It feels funny, gonna have it analyzed."

"Good, let me know what you find, Ok?"

"Sure, I'll just pass it to Tom."

Once everyone was out, I met back up with Agent Thomas.

"Mr. Kelly, I appreciate your help. I'll see what I can do on my part. There is an Agent on his way from DC. He is going to be taking over this case. I just got the word on that. I will be sure to let him know how you helped us."

"Thanks."

After they left, the rest of us stood around outside smoking and talking about nothing. The shit around there was getting worse. Someone had actually gotten hurt. Things had changed. After about half an hour, I sent everyone home.

After dinner Hank told me

"Chief that was more like a mission, than anything else."

"Sure was, actually felt like we had something to fight."

"Well, it's something anyway."

Later I watched Bailey get into bed in her own nightclothes. I had a new vision for my dreams

Tim Hancock

August 11

For the second day in a row, the FBI was
waiting for us, when we pulled in the gate.
The car was a rental.

"Must be the guy from DC." Bailey gave me a
nervous smile.

"Should I call the lawyers again?"

I laughed. "Not just yet."

I parked next to the rental. I was more than a
little surprised, when Ed Watkins got out.
He'd put on a few, maybe twenty, pounds since
I'd last seen him.

"Good to see you again Brian." We *had* had a
beer somewhere on the circle.

"Wish I could say the same Ed."

"Ma'am, Brian, we need to go somewhere and
talk."

I motioned toward the Main building. His look
told me he'd been well briefed.

"We've got a makeshift office in the back of
the command center."

"Something a little more private Brian."

196

"My place is five minutes from here. You can ride with us."

"Brian, this is…"

"Ed whatever you tell me, she's gonna know anyway."

"Let's go then."

Once we were in the car, he opened his case.

"It's been fifty years. This stuff is a little old."

"Ed, it's still brand new to him."

"Him?"

"Go on."

"Here's not the best place."

"It's a good place to start."

"It's a long story old friend."

"Wait then, we're almost there anyway."

We got to my place and took a pot of coffee out by the pool.

"Ok Ed, we're all comfortable, and this is private. Let's hear it."

"I'll start in…"

"Ed, your fuckin stalling."

The doorbell rang. To my surprise Ed said. "Better let me get that."

He came back about a minute later, with a rather old looking guy.

"Brian Kelly, Bailey Kirkwood, meet Stewart Kensington. He is going to help me tell my story Brian. After yesterday, my superiors thought you needed to know everything." I got a chair for the old man.

"I'll start. Mr. Kensington, you can fill in the pieces as we go."

"The Tulsa facility, of the foundation, was built specifically for final human testing of experimental performance enhancement procedures. Mostly drug induced. Jacob Harris was assigned as the Managing Director. He was really a front for Dr. Kensington."

"I was the founder of the Foundation." "Jacob really had no Idea. Why don't you just let me Mr. Watkins? I think I can handle it."

I was glad, information from the source, not something Ed had read.

"Go on Mr. Kensington."

"Stewart, please. I have not been called Mr. Kensington in years. Jacob was just an administrator, and not a very good one. We did a lot of cover research, but the real stuff went on downstairs. We knew that we would lose some people. We knew some would not handle the treatment well. That's the reason we kept them in cells."

"At first, I was too busy, with three facilities, To handle everything. We had a project that we were building up to. We had been working on a way to make people disappear. It was developed in Philadelphia, and then sent to Dallas for animal testing. We were trying to phase them. A way to send troops in undetected."

"A-21?"

"Yes, A-21. I started hearing things. Bad things were happening down here. Some of our scientists had begun using their own drugs. Even giving it to the staff. Things were out of control. I had to come, to take over myself. I waited too long. I felt it was more important to wait, until we could transfer A-21 from Dallas. I knew I needed to be with it, when it was being tested. We had some success on the small model, with rats and such. The big one was being built in Dallas."

"One of the scientists, a man I trusted, had taken charge of things up here. I swear to you, I didn't know. I didn't know that Samuel was that bad. I found out when I got here."

"I read his files. He was taking his own drugs. "Giving them to the girls in the typing pool. Turning them, in to his playthings. Making them do horrible, despicable things."

"I should have shut the whole thing down right then. I tried. They would not let me. They said I could after A-21 was operational. That's why I agreed to continue. Then, that damn accident in Dallas."

"We were two days away from the final test. I got a call from the director in Dallas. The small unit, the one we called M-15, had messed up. We lost an entire lab full of Doctors and research assistants. I had to go. Twenty people had vanished, I had to go."

"By then A-21 was set to go." "I told them it was on hold until I got back. A-21 would become A-23. I told them not to do it. I went to Dallas."

"The people were not gone from the lab. They

were not in it either. They were part of it.
It was different there. The Labs were separate
buildings. God help us we tried to burn the
building. We couldn't. It just wouldn't burn.
We gave it some help Lots of fuel. It finally
worked. I can still hear their screams."

"Back here, they didn't wait. Samuel did the
test with out me. It went horribly wrong here
too, only, on a much larger scale."

"That I know of, only one person, who was in
that building on August 21, 1942, got out
alive. Somehow he managed to hide. He was
there, waiting for me, when I got back."

"He was one of the test subjects, an Army
Sargent. He told me the story. There were a
few that were not affected by the test. The
rest were absorbed into the building. Those
were his exact words. He told me he could hear
their voices in his head. Then he could hear
only one, Samuel Brady."

"Samuel had gotten control of the building,
physical control. He could make it do things.
He was also in control of the people in the
building. This young Sargent told me he could
hear Samuel telling them what to do. He almost
did it himself. The only thing I can
contribute to his ability to resist, were the
drugs he had been given."

I looked at Bailey. She gave me a reassuring
smile.

"He said Samuel forced these people into the
cells in the basement. Then he used the gas
heaters and turned the whole basement into a
furnace."

"He cooked those people?"

"Incinerated them is the more precise word young lady. I hid the Sargent in the shed, behind my home and called the Army."

"A few days later they came and took us both away." "I don't know what happened after that."

"I would not be here talking to you about this now, if Samuel had not called me after you moved in. He found me somehow, after all of these years. He told me he had some new playthings. That is when I called you Mr. Kelly."

Ed offered the rest of the story. "The Sargent committed suicide a year later. He couldn't live with what he had witnessed. The Army sent some people to destroy the building. They doused it with gasoline and Diesel fuel. "It burned for hours."

"When the flames cleared the building stood. It was charred black, but it was mostly undamaged. Two soldiers were lost in the attempt. Official report says they were most likely trapped in the fire."

"The building was locked and forgotten. It was sold, by accident in 1962. It was passed to Mr. Earnest Prescott in the early seventies and left untouched, until you got it earlier this year."

"That is about all there is to know about this. The government has kept a lid on this for fifty years Brian. I have convinced my superiors and the Army you will use this information with discretion."

"I need to add a few more things Mr. Kelly. Samuel Brady is Evil Incarnate. He most likely was before this incident. I was touched by the place when I came back from Dallas. I can feel the pull again, now that I am so close. I can not stay much longer."

"You, and those around you have been touched also. None of you will be completely safe, as long as he is part of that building."

"Why do you suppose, Mr. Kelly, that you have yet to abandon it completely. Even knowing what you know now, you still plan to wait and see."

The old man stood. He touched my arm.

"You know what must be done Brian. Do it soon, for her sake."

"Ed, make sure he gets on the plane."

"Have no fear Brian, after what the agents told me yesterday, he will be escorted directly there. He told me this morning he was having trouble resisting the call."

"Now, you have the information you wanted, what do you plan to do."

"I plan to think, let my people know what's going on, and then we will act."

"I will be seeing you Brian."

"Nice to meet you Miss. Kirkwood."

I let him show himself to the door.

"Bailey call everyone, I want them here within the hour. Have Bruiser make sure to get two patrol people to stay with the dispatcher."

"Bri, can all of that be true?"

"It sure fits."

She went to the den to make some the calls. I closed my eyes. I let the story I'd been told become a movie in my mind. It was almost too improbable. Yet it made perfect sense. Suddenly, I wanted very much not to be alone. I went in search of Bailey. I wanted to be with her the most, but anyone would have worked at that moment.

We sat in the den with the admin workers, safety in numbers, until the others arrived. I got them together, back out by the pool. By the time I had finished my story it was getting dark.

They all had their comments; most were not worth repeating. We all agreed that we needed everything out of that building as soon as possible.

Bailey said she would get working on having things set up so our move on the 15th would be easy as possible. Our biggest hitches, were all of the inventory in the bay and of course the command post. We agreed that we would work out a plan in the morning.

We adjourned and Most went home. Hank and Shay stayed at my place again that night. My two bedroom, two bath with den, was quickly becoming a family home. I missed my parents real bad for some reason. Hank and I stayed by the pool for awhile.

"Chief, all that stuff I said, about giving up."

" Forget it Hank."

"No, Chief, I wont forget it. I was wrong, we

should have left then."

"We couldn't Hank. We still cant. Not until I can help Shawn"

When Bailey and I went to bed, I realized how nice it was to have someone there with me. Someone to love, someone to touch and to hold. That's all it was, for now that was enough.

August 12

As agreed, we met at my place the next morning. My pool deck had become our new base of operations. We could have met in my dining room or living room, but they were too close to the den.

Bailey and Shay had made a hell of a breakfast spread. They served it up, buffet style. Everyone heaped it on and we sat down for our round table.

"What ever we decide, we can't do until we get the command post moved. Anyone have any ideas on that one?"

Ken said "The problem is chief, we can't move it anywhere until we get the lines moved."

Ice added, "That can take at least two to three days, even longer for the T-1's. We need to have one ready when we take the other down. Normally, it would take about three weeks to get something like that done. Sound about right Ken?"

"Sounds right, how much time do we have?"

"We get the keys to the new place Monday."

"Three days, and that's a weekend to boot."
"What'd you think Ice?"

"I don't see it working."

Bailey offered some hope. "The Phone Company said they would have all the phones available, at all locations, by noon Monday. The problem is the new T-1's. The can't have them active until Tuesday, at the earliest."

"Ice, can we do dialup until then?"

"Yes, we can do it, if the phone lines are decent. But you're talking 9600 baud on a system that needs ten times that."

"It'll work, just be slow as shit." Ken added, "If the lines are decent."

"Ok, if we can do that, how long to get everything set up?"

"Depends on what's available. Ken and I can get it all done, even if we have to run all new lines, by Monday night."

"What if we get some of our installers working with you?"

"Damn chief, I was already figuring that into the time frame."

"Monday Night?"

"Yeah chief, we have everything we need, but we still gotta get it out."

"Good point Hank. We need to get everything out of there."

"Chief we got least four loads a shit in the bay alone. How we gonna get all that outta there? That's gonna take a lot of time and a lot a people."

"I know Gunner, and we still don't have a place to put it. Bailey I need a couple of things. Find me moving vans with drivers and loaders. Also a local mini-storage, we need as many units as they can get, close together."

She smiled. "That's the easy part. Brand new one opened Monday, just down the road. When do you want the trucks Bri."

"Today too soon?"

She sighed deep; "I'll see what I can do."

"Ok for now everybody go to work. Bailey, one more thing sweetie, call the leasing agent. See if she can get Ken and Ice in to the ops building to check it out."

"Anything else, " she teased, "I think I have a small empty spot on my plate."

"Sorry babe, you're the best."

"Flattery will get you nowhere, I want money."

Everyone was getting busy. I drove to the bus. I was surprised to see the Caddy and Ambulance sitting out front. It took awhile but I remembered they had been getting dressed up. The caddy looked pretty cool with the decal and light bar. The ambulance was painted like all of our patrol cars. It had seemed like a good idea, at the time. Now, it seemed pointless.

Bruiser, Tom and Gunner were admiring them when I parked.

"What a waste, huh guys?"

"What'd ya mean by that Chief?"

"Bruiser they're a part of this place, we can't take them with us."

"I see yer point. Still they look good."

"Sure do, let's get em put in the garages."

Tom drove the caddy and Bruiser took the ambulance. I let them take each for a quick run. I even drove the ambulance, just once, for the hell of it. We backed em in their spots. The old lettering already starting to show through on the Ambulance.

I went to my makeshift office. I kept thinking about what the old man had said. How we were drawn to it. It dawned on me that we had made every decision this morning, except what we were going to do about the buildings. *"…Even knowing what you know now, you still want to wait and see…"*

He was right, why shouldn't he be. He had dealt with it for fifty years. The phone rang; I knew who it was. Because Bruiser, Gunner and Tom were there with me I put it on the speaker.

"Brian Kelly."

"Good afternoon Brian."

"It's been awhile, forget my number?"

"Still a smartass, is that right Brian."

"Well Samuel, I am what I am."

"Trying to shock me Brian, not this time. I knew Stewart was near, I felt him. I guess he told you everything."

"He told me a lot Sammy."

"Must you be so disrespectful Brian? You know how that angers me."

"Point is, I don't' really give a fuck, old boy. Here's the thing Samuel, I'm going to get my stuff out of you, then you can rot."

"I'm afraid I can't allow you to do that Brian."

"Just how do you plan to stop me Samuel?"

"I still have a few tricks up my sleeve Brian. You have not seen my best work. See Bri, I can't have you trying something stupid, like trying to burn me. That was a pathetic attempt by the Army, the first time. I am too strong for that. That did nothing, but allow me to claim two more."

"Samuel, I will do whatever it takes to remove my property. I know how to cause you pain."

"Yes, you do, so barbaric."

"You have the nerve to call me barbaric, you sick twisted fuck. Your such a limp dick, you had to drug women to fuck you. You were inadequate, as a scientist and a man. In my honest opinion, you're pathetic as a building too." "I guess that makes you a three time loser."

Voice change. "Why, do you insist, on pissing me off? You have no idea what I am capable of you arrogant prick. At first, I wanted you gone all of you, now you are a part of me as well. I am never going to let you go." "You can't fucking destroy me Brian, I WILL destroy you."

"The best thing about you Sammy, I can shut you up." I hung up.

Tom looked at me across the table. "That guy has some issues."

His expression never changed, but I laughed in

spite of myself.

Gunner added, "Issues, hell, that motherfucker's way gone."

Bailey called on my cell. "Bri, I have got four trucks and twelve loaders coming first thing tomorrow. The Mini Storage place said all of their units are open. We can have whatever we need."

"You do great work, remind me to hug you."

"If I have to remind you, it isn't worth it. Best part, the leasing agent is meeting Ken and Ice at the Ops office. She gave me the key to the other one today. The girls and I are going to get the stuff moved over there now. No phones yet, but it's Friday so we will make do. You get your den back."

"You're wonderful Bailey, I love you."

"I love you too Bri." "See you at home."

"Yeah, I'll be there soon." "Everyone meets at my place at six. Bring your wives and girlfriends. Plan to get wet, dress accordingly spread the word."

As I walked out I leaned over the dispatchers desk. "Mandy, that means you too." Bruiser beamed.

As I walked to my car, the side door opened on it's own.

"Go fuck yourself" "I'm not playing with you tonight."

I drove home in a better mood. We were going to need some fun tonight, the weekend, as they say, was gonna be a bitch.

Word had gotten out. Everyone was there. Ken's wife was back in town and making a rare appearance. She didn't socialize much since her stroke, but she looked good.

I cornered Bailey in the kitchen.

"This whole thing was just a sham to get you back in that bikini again."

She blushed. "So sorry to disappoint you Mr. Kelly, but as you can see I am wearing shorts and a T-shirt."

"You plan to wear that in the pool."

She blushed again, and smiled sweetly. "No, I bought a new red one, Hope you like it. Hey Bri. I hope you don't mind, I asked Paige, one of our office girls, to stop by."

"Bailey, why would I mind that?"

"She's kinda sweet on Ice."

"I see. Playing matchmaker?"

"No, not really, I just figured with everything that was going on, he could use a… Damn, what was the word?" "Oh I remember. Distraction!" She walked away, leaving me just a bit stung.

As it turned out, Ice welcomed the distraction. Paige was cute, which didn't hurt any. She was a bit too peppy and giddy for me, but she practically doted on Ice. He ate it up. It was good to see him happy. At least his mind was off Shawn.

Soon enough, people gravitated to the pool. Apparently Bailey and Shay had gone shopping together. Their new suites were identical. In pink Bailey was beautiful, in a sweet innocent, girl next door way. In red she was stunning. It was the difference in color and cut. She still looked sweet, but the innocence was replaced by sexy.

At her worst, Bailey was a treasure to look at. Always attractive and regardless of what she was wearing, she was desirable. Simply sexy, was not the thought she usually provoked. This was different.

Finally our guests gone and Hank and Shay in their room. Bailey and I were alone. She had put on a light cotton cover-up and was back to sweet and innocent. We were sitting on the leather loveseat in my freshly reacquired den.

"Forgive me for saying this but, God you looked hot tonight."

She blushed again, reaffirming her true innocence. She slid closer, her back to me, and laid her head back on my shoulder.

"Bri, do you want me as much as I do you?" The question shocked me.

"Honestly Bailey, probably even more."

"I have thought about it a lot, have since we met. You were married then. The truth is, I'm not ready yet. I love our closeness Bri, sometimes I want more, but I'm scared. I'm not scared of the act, I'm scared of the change."

"Bailey, my love, what we have now is better than anything I've ever known, that will never change. If and when you get ready, I'll be here."

"I love you Bri."

"I love you too."

We slept right there, just like that. I had
visions of her again, but she was wearing a
long white dress. That night was the last
night we were all together. Away from the
building.

Part 3 Moving Again (The Final Days)

August 13 & 14

The nine of us met on the loading dock at seven-thirty. We needed to get some things ready before the movers showed up.

The good thing, everything was already in boxes. The Bad thing, it was all in the bay. We had our usual list of emergency equipment, torch, shotguns, flashlights and axes. I had added a few things to the list for today.

I bought four large pry bars, four C-clamps, two crosscut saws, a hacksaw and two 12" chainsaws, fueled and ready. We had two of the overhead doors open and the C-clamps in place, ensuring they would stay that way.

Ice and me were inside cutting the fronts off of the cages containing our equipment. The rest were outside, waiting for the trucks.

"How you holdn up Steve?"

"I get by chief. I miss Shawn, but I'm glad he's safe. Last night helped." I didn't miss the smile.

"Paige?"

"Man, she's somethin, cute as hell."

"You guys hang out after the party?"

He gave me a sideways look. "Yeah, went back to my place. We talked forever. Brian, I never spent the whole night, just talking with a girl."

"Try getting married, it's ALL you'll do."

"Best part is, I can't wait to do the same thing again."

We were half finished.

"Gonna see her again?"

"Yep, tonight. Brian, can I ask you something?"

"Sure, go ahead."

"It's about you and Bailey."

"We got nothin to hide, ask away."

"It looks like you guys got it all, man. I mean you two are close. I know she stays at your place a lot. It just don't seem like you guys are, well you know."

The guy was observant.

"It's complicated. No, we're not. Yes, it's the best relationship I've ever been in."

He sighed heavily. "That's what I'm talkin about."

"Better than your marriage. Bad comparison Ice. Better than my engagement."

"What happened with you and Carol?"

He was getting personal, but he was looking for advice, not being nosey.

"I didn't give her enough."

"Enough what?"

"Time, attention, Money."

"Money?"

"That was Carol, Ice, she wanted money, more than anything else."

"At least you didn't have kids."

"That would have required having sex, that's one thing she didn't want much. She's married, again, livin in Tampa."

"Guy loaded?"

"Yeah, some kinda broker."

"They got kids?"

"Not yet."

He laughed. "Guess he ain't getting none either."

We were on the last cage; I could hear the trucks outside.

"So far ho good, huh Ice" He looked around.

"Yep, looks like any other warehouse."

We finished and went out with the rest. Hank had all of the loaders and drivers off to one side waiting for me.

I had made up a story for them, no point in trying the truth. I lit a smoke and walked to them.

"Mornin folks, I'm Brian Kelly. This is a government special projects facility. Inside there are about forty or so storage cages with the fronts removed. The materials that are in those cages are the only things we will be moving today. Since this is an access-restricted facility, I must ask you not to enter any of the other cages. If you need to use the facilities, get with one of my people."

"It is very important, that you don't wander off on your own. If you start feeling strange, sick, dizzy, lightheaded, or if you see something unusual, find me, or one of my people immediately. If you start feeling strange and for some reason can't find one of my people, tell someone on your crew. If someone does come to you, or you notice them acting strange, get them out of the building, then find one of us."

"This is for your safety and the security of this facility. Are there any questions?"

They had em, but they didn't know how to ask. "Alright then, give me a minute with my staff and we'll get started."

"Keep an eye on them. I don't know what to expect. If they have to piss, take them to the bus. If things get weird get them out."

As planned, we broke them up in two teams. Three of our people were on each of those teams. Bailey and Shay stayed on the dock. I stayed where I could watch most of it.

The guys were pro's. They may get paid by the hour, but the company gets it by the load. Within an hour, they'd emptied eleven cages and filled one truck. At the rate they were going, I figured we would be done in about two and a half more hours.

I went out on the dock and lit another smoke. Bailey took it, so I lit another.

"So far so good, Bri."

"I know, it's strange. I figured we'd have a fight on our hands."

"We're not done yet."

She was right, I went back to the doorway. *"He's waitin for the right time. Waiting for us to let our guard down."* I knew somethin was gonna happen, I just didn't know when.

When, came about two hours later. We had three trucks full and three cages left. Several things happened about the same time. It all happened faster than we could handle.

The door to A-21 opened, one of the loaders went in and the door closed. Another of the workers saw it happen, he started to follow him, but remembered what I'd said. He only remembered part of it. Instead of finding one of us, he went looking for his supervisor.

The doors to the hole flew open. Another of the shimmers came out and ran full force into one of the loaders, knocking him on his ass.

At the same time, I saw another worker going through the door to the pool. I saw it, but it didn't register.

This started us moving. Ken and Tom went to the fallen worker, helping him up and leading him out of the building. Hank, Gunner, Bruiser and I ran to the hole and closed the doors. Almost closed them, is more correct. As soon as we got them shut, they flew open again, with enough force to throw the four of us twenty feet. During my flight I yelled.

"EVERYONE GET THE FUCK OUT!"

Ice, who had just loaded our last gun safe on the truck, missed what happened but heard my shout. So did Bailey and Shay, on the dock. Bailey started inside but Shay stopped her.

"No honey, we stay here."

She was still pissed when she told me about it, much later.

Ice did come in and started rushing everyone out the doors. Two more shimmers came out of the hole, but they missed their targets and evaporated in the sunlight.

When everyone was out of the bay, I went to the supervisor.

"Get a head count. We got one of yours in the bus."

"What-n-the hell was that Mr. Kelly."

"One of the things I warned you about,"

"My guy gonna be ok?"

"He's gonna have to see a doctor, but he'll back on his feet soon. Get your head count."

"Hank, we got a guy in the main building."
"We're gonna have to go get him. Shay, you and Bailey go back to the bus and take over for Ken. Send him and Tom out here. Call Doug, his numbers in my Rolodex, tell him I got another one, ask him what to do."

Hank, Ice, Gunner, Bruiser and I went to the side entrance. Ken and Tom met us there.

"I saw a guy go in, just as all hell broke

loose. Might be not be related, but I think it is. Let's go get em."

When we went in through the door, we saw him. He was standing in the middle of the pool.

"You ok?"

"Uh, well, I can't move."

"Why not?"

He started to move and a desk slid to stop him.

"Every time I try to move, that happens. I already got a couple bad bruises."

"What are you doing in here?"

"Your speech made me curious. Figured I'd slip in when no one was lookin."

"Hank said, "I'll get ya buddy."

When he stepped forward a desk, moving faster than most cars on the interstate hit him from the side. He went down.

"I'm ok chief. Son-of –bitch."

He got up, but he was hurt. My cell started ringing.

"Kelly."

"Brian," Mr. far away voice said, "what do we have here?"

"Samuel, leave him alone. He's got nothin to do with this."

"Maybe he don't Bri, but he's here isn't he?"

"What the fuck do you want."

"What I've always wanted. I want my life, my freedom back."

"It's too fuckin late for that Samuel. You made that choice fifty years ago."

"Oh but you see, I had it for awhile, but you took it away."

"Shawn."

"Very good Brian. Now I have another, until you whores take him away too. It takes so much of me to do that Brian, and you made me waste them. Now I want you. Go in the basement Brian." "Do that, and I'll let this worthless piece of trash go."

"And if I don't?"

"At the very least, those desks will cripple him."

"I have a better Idea."

I had been giving subtle signals to the guys. I hoped they got them. I hoped they remembered. \

"What's that Bri?"

"This!"

I threw the phone to Hank. Bruiser fired the shotgun in to the closest desk. I ran as hard as I could. My right knee sending lightning bolts in protest. I jumped onto one of the desks. Still running, I dived for the loader. I caught him under the arms and lifted, springing again over the desk behind him. I never stopped moving. I threw him through the fire exit door.

Ken and Gunner had gone out. When I turned around to face the pool, they came back in, with the chainsaws. Hank tossed the phone back to me.

"How's that asshole?"

The other voice answered. "Think your fucking smart. You think you did something?"

"I think I got him away from you."

"Him, yes. Do you really think I'm fucking stupid Brian? Let me tell you a secrete asshole, I got another fuckin little birdie. By the time you find this one, it will be too late."

I hung up the phone. "Out back guys, let's move."

I went out the fire exit and the worker was still there.

"What the fuck was that?"

"Just an experiment, that's why I told you guys to follow directions. Man, I never saw anyone move like that. How'd you do it?"

"It's part of my training. Let's get you back with your guys."

When we got to the back, I went to the Supervisor.

"Mr. Kelly, I'm still missing one. This here's Jack, he's got something to tell ya."

"Ah, Mr. Kelly, sir, I seen Mickey go in one of them cages. Figured he was lookin for sumthin ta steel. I went lookin fer Mr. Morgan. Figured he'd get Mickey, but kinda keep him outta trouble. It was bout the time all this other stuff happened."

"Which cage, Jack?"

"That one wit the boards all on it."

"God help us." "Ok, Jack. We'll take care of it."

From the looks of the guys, they had heard.

"Bring everything."

We went back in to the bay. It was pretty quiet. The doors to the hole were still open, waiting. I tried the easy way first. The 9-mm round sent the lock across the bay floor. The door still wouldn't open.

"Hey Mickey, you in there?"

I could hear muffled sounds, but got no answer.

"Ice get the door off, make it quick."

Ice started on one side of the cage. Hank was on the other side with the hacksaw. The noises from the cage got louder, it sounded like he was kicking his feet.

"He's choking!"

I grabbed a chainsaw from Ken, started it, took it to full throttle and buried it in the front of the cage. The saw complained loudly and it bucked like a bull, but it was cutting through. Gunner had the other saw and started in too.

Before long we had a good size hole in the front of the cage. I could see Mickey. A cable, from somewhere, had wound around his neck. It was killing him. Several of us tried to pull it off. All we were doing was buying time.

I pulled my nine and handed it to Gunner. He was the only one I trusted with the shot. He fired once and the cable snapped. We got

Mickey up and out of there.

"Call him an ambulance."

We pulled the C-clamps and closed the doors. I was exhausted.

"Mr. Morgan, your guys are gonna be alright. We are done for the day. You can take your trucks and unload them. Some of my guys will meet you there. Bruiser, you and Gunner can take care of that."

"Got it chief."

"Ken, what do we have left in there?"

"Nothing we can't replace."

"Good enough. Let's check on the other guy. Hank, you ok."

"Gonna hurt for awhile, but yeah, I'm ok."

We hurried back to the bus.

"Shay, what did Doug say?"

"He gave me the name of a doctor down here. He said he would call him and tell him what to do. Guy runs a private hospital. They are sending a car for him now. Doug told me to give him some Valium. He said one of mine was ok. I gave him that and one of Baileys pills to be safe."

"Good job. Shay, Hank's hurt a little, check on him."

It didn't take her a second. She took him in the head and checked him over good. She was back quick.

"Chief, I'm takin him to the doc, just to be safe."

"Ok Shay, keep me posted. Ice, ready to follow your true calling again?"

"You want me to blow something up?"

"Soon Ice, Soon."

Bailey took my arm. "What are you planning to do Bri?"

"I'm gonna end it. Ice, do the math. Let me know what you need. When we're done, I don't want a piece big enough to hide a cockroach."

"Gonna take a few days. Hell, it's Gonna take a shit load of stuff."

"Get it, I'll pay for it, no matter the cost."

"I'll get started."

 I sat in the back of the bus, collecting my thoughts. Bailey stood behind me, rubbing my shoulders.

"What's next?"

"We need to get the other offices up, then I'll take care of this place."

"What are you planning?"

"I'm going to level it, I got no choice."

"I guess not. You think that'll end it?"

"I hope so."

"Ready to go home?"

"Yeah, You think we should empty the other offices?"

"Not now, maybe Monday."

"Guess so, let's go home."

Tom was waiting for us outside. "Hey Brian,

got a sec?"

"Sure Tom."

"I'll wait for you in the car."

"No, Bailey wait. I want to talk to you too."

"What's up Tom?"

"Brian, I can't do this any more. I'm done. I talked to my wife about it. Now, after this shit today. I just can't do it anymore."

"You sure about this Tom."

"Yeah, I'm sure."

I couldn't make him stay. I couldn't even bring myself to try. After everything that had happened, I couldn't think of a convincing argument.

"Ok, Tom, we're here if you need anything."

"Thanks Brian, you too Bailey."

"Keep in touch Tom."

He walked away, headed for his car.

"Sorry Bri."

"Yeah, me too."

We drove home, not talking much. Once we got home, I told Hank and Shay about Tom.

"So, what did the Doc say?"

"Not much, just bruised a bit. Nothing is broken. It's too bad about Tom man. So what happens now chief?"

"Monday, we get the rest of the stuff out of the building. Then, once everything is set up, we move the bus. Then, I level the place."

"Gonna take some doin."

"Yeah, I got Ice on it."

"Gonna be some fireworks."

"Say Hank, what say we take those ladies out to the boat?"

"Tonight?"

"Sure, we can spend the night on the boat and make a day of it tomorrow."

"Sounds good to me."

"Let's ask them."

They agreed so we packed some stuff and made the hour drive to Pier 51 Marina. By the time we got unpacked we were exhausted. I put Hank and Shay in the front cabin. Bailey and I took the Aft one.

We sat out on the deck drinking some beers and talking. It was nice and relaxing. We went to bed late. I slept till noon.

We spent the next day out on the lake. The fact that none of us got a call or page was reassuring. We docked the boat around five and drove back to the city. We decided to make an early night of it. We were going to be real busy the next couple of days.

Before I went to bed I called Bruiser, just to check. He told me everything had been quiet. "Nothin at all happening here." I went to sleep, thinking ahead, about the coming days.

August 15 & 16

I followed Bailey to our new administration
office. It was a seven-office suite. We
decided to base the Admin and sales office
here.

Ken and Shay would also have their offices
here. I was lucky enough to have an office in
both places. The sales guys were in the
process of moving their stuff from the hotel.
It was only nine, but the phones were already
on. One of our install techs was busy getting
them set up.

Bailey had called Court Furniture Rental. They
had most of the office stuff already here.
They were sending another truck, to the other
location. The leasing agent met us there and
gave me the keys to the new Operations
offices.

I met Ice and Ken at that building less than
an hour later. The story was pretty much the
same there. This was a nine-office suite with
a reception area and a check-in desk. This
area was perfect for the dispatchers office.

It already had the counters set up. Ice had checked it out a few days earlier.

"This place's almost perfect. Most of the phone switching stuff's already here. We're gonna put in redundant systems in dispatch so we can run two people. I got all the techs here and at admin. Hopefully, we can get all this done today. Just figure on havin the day girl here in the morning."

"Good, then we can get that bus back to the PD."

"Guess Tom didn't tell you, we bought that."

"Ok, well guess we can find a place to keep it, till we need it."

"What you got planned today chief?"

"Hank, Gunner, Bruiser and me are gonna get some of the patrol guys to help us move stuff here and to the admin building."

"You ain't goin in there are ya?" "Nah, just gonna get the vehicles and stuff today. Probably get the things out of the bus. I figured we'd all go empty the building tomorrow."

"Good, don't think you need to be in there, without all of us."

Ken came from the back. "Chief, I wanna show you a couple of things. First, you get the big office in the back."

"Damn thing's huge."

"This room here next to it's the break room. "What none of us noticed, was the conference room, It's between the two. You have to be in one of them, to get to it. That's what I wanted show you."

He opened the door. It was already set up with a big table and fourteen chairs.

"Home of the weekly staff meeting?"

"Yeah Ken, this will work."

"Ok, well I gotta get busy."

"Ok, let's all get together here about five."

"See ya then."

I drove to the building and met with Hank. We spent most of the rest of the day shuttling between there and the two new locations. About four thirty, the lot was empty and the bus was damn near.

"Anything left we can get out after we move it tomorrow. Let's go have a meeting with everyone else. Tomorrow should prove to be a shit load of fun."

At five fifteen we were all gathered around the conference table.

"How'd things go today?"

Bailey went first. "The admin office is all set. I have no problems at all there. We are getting good response to our employment ads and you guys have interviews, starting Wednesday."

"Great, anything else?"

Ken was next. "I only have one thing to add. It's good news. We got a couple of great new contracts today. One's for an office building, the other is big, for a gated community. We got everything, from access control, to patrols. We are going to need more installers and guards soon. Ice can fill you in on things here."

"Sure, everything here is set. One of my techs used to work for the Phone Company and he got the T-1's rushed. They are up and running. We could've moved everything here tonight. It'll be easier to start with the day shift. We got a system set up at admin." "Didn't figure we needed on here."

"No, I agree, no need for that."

"Other than that, everything's set here."

"Good, anything else?" everyone was quiet. "Ok, now it's my turn."

"Tomorrow, we get the rest of our stuff outta the old building. I'm getting a thirty footer from U-Haul. I figure we can load everything in it and the bus. I don't want to waste any time in that building. We get what we brought, and get out. We'll do the break and bunkroom's first. Then we'll do our offices."

"Anything that is permanently installed stays." "If you don't want it or need it, leave it. I'll replace anything that's left. Ice, how's your shopping list coming?"

"Got most of what I need, the rest is gonna take a few days."

"Fair enough, when it's ready let me know. I need someone to hang out here tomorrow, to make sure things get going good."

I had no volunteers. Everyone wanted to be a part of the move.

"Bruiser, you're elected. Let's go home and get some rest, it's gonna be a long day tomorrow. Meet at the bus at nine."

Hank and Shay had dinner with Bailey and me, then went back to their place. Bailey and I watched TV in the den. I feel asleep with my head in her lap. Wondering again what the next day would bring.

She woke me at seven. I was still on the loveseat. We had breakfast with Hank and Shay at the Village Inn. They drove me to get the U-Haul and then followed me to the Bus.

It was eight-thirty but everyone was early. Ken and Ice in one half ton, Gunner in the other. Ice and Ken had already disconnected the bus and it was ready to move.

Gunner had gotten all of the files out of it. I planned on returning them to the pool. We had our usual equipment ready. The torch was in the truck. I didn't figure we'd need it. Ken had a big pair of cable cutters.

"Some things I'd rather not leave."

"Let's do this."

I didn't want to have to bother with the outside doors, so we removed them. The building, or Samuel, started as soon as we walked in. The door to the bay opened. We ignored it. Desks moved to block our way. We cut three in half before it, he, got the point. We finally got to the other side of the pool.

We split into two groups. One group took the bunkroom. The other took the break room. We had them packed in no time.

"We fill the U-Haul first. If we need more

room, start on the half tons."

We carried boxes out the back door, dodging the occasional flying object. *"I can't believe he's throwin shit at us."* We had to stop, for a bit, when Gunner didn't see a desk drawer headed his way and took it in the back. He was all right so we finished up in the bay area.

Ken and Ice retrieved the recorders, and anything else they felt useful, from the booth. About noon, we were done with the downstairs completely.

Bailey and shay made a burger run. We had lunch in the bus, making plans for the upstairs.

There were only a few offices that had much in them. Bruiser, Gunner and Ice never really moved in. We took care of those and Tom and Shawn's offices first.

Bailey and Ken had emptied their offices when we moved sales and Admin. That only left mine, Hanks and Shays.

"We do one office at a time. Lets try to keep two people in the hall. These are small spaces, be ready for anything."

We packed and emptied the first four offices, without much resistance. In Shawn's office things got a bit worse. He hadn't moved a lot in there. Picture's of him and Ice, their departed parents and their sister and her family and some general office stuff.

Ice and Ken were in there packing; the rest of us were in the hall. The door started to shut on it's own and I moved to stop it. The desk slid quickly, trapping Ice between it and the wall. Ken and Hank tried to move it, but it wouldn't budge.

Gunner fired up one of the saws. Before he could get to the desk the file cabinet flew across the room, barely missing him.

Instead of cutting the desk, he dug the saw into the wall. Hank was then able to move the desk. We finished Shawn's office pretty quick after that.

The story was pretty much the same in Hank and Shay's offices. We managed to get them packed and loaded in the truck. The day was beginning to fade when we started on the final office, mine.

Unfortunately, thanks to Bailey, my office had been well decorated. To add to the problem, we had to have most of the files. I looked at the huge desk. Man I don't want thing on one of us.

We started with the files. We had to pry the drawers open. The front came off one, so that was even harder. Once we got the file cabinet packed, the black phone started ringing. The others were packing stuff from the walls and desktop. I answered the call.

"Good evening Samuel"

"Brian, please, reconsider, for your sake."

"For my sake?"

"I can't let you leave me alone again Brian."

"How do you plan to stop me?"

"You see, Brian, before you came, I had to make do."

"Make do?"

"With the occasional homeless person or runaway. They would wonder in, I'd play with them. They were all weak. Once in awhile one would get away. Most of them bored me. Those ended up in my basement. You are going to force me to do that again. If you hadn't hurt me Brian, if you had not taken so much of me away, we could have existed here peacefully, together."

I let him talk. I was trying to keep him busy, while the others packed.

"Samuel, you made the first move, I believe."

"No, I was just playing a bit. Until you started changing things, and taking things away. Until you started snooping around."

"I have a business to run Samuel. We had to change things to suit our purpose."

"It suited me fine!"

"But I didn't know anything about that."

"Brian, do you know what it's like to have part of you removed? Cut away with no anesthesia. I felt everything you did. I am sure you are aware of that by now."

"I am, Now!"

"Yet, you continue to cause me pain." "Only when you make it necessary."

They were almost finished packing. Some of them had started carrying things out.

"I made nothing necessary." He was getting excited. "I only wanted to keep what was mine."

235

"What are you trying to keep now?"

"You, all of you. You don't bore me. I don't want to be alone again. Do you have any idea what it is like to be alone, for almost fifty years."

"Samuel, you really need to work on your people skills. The way you've acted isn't the best way to win friends and influence people."

"Your feeble attempt at humor is lost on me Brian. I can not let you leave me alone again. I will call you each time I take another homeless person. They, will be on your head, Brian."

My office was empty except for Hank, Gunner, Ken and I.

"Samuel, I promise I will visit you."

"Visit me?" "Sure, I'll visit you soon."

"That is very nice. I see you have gotten all of your things."

"Yes Samuel, I'll see you again soon. We will talk then."

"Brian, you are a man of your word?"

"Of course Samuel."

"You promise to visit me?"

"I do."

"Then I will not hinder your departure in any way." "That's civil of you."

"Brian, before you go there is something I must tell you." He was silent for a minute. "Never mind for now." "Good day Brian."

I hung up the phone and we all walked you to

the trucks."

"Ken take the bus and park it behind the operations building. The rest of us will meet you there."

"Bri, the building, it looks peaceful. What happened?" "I promised to visit again soon." I couldn't help but wonder what he had wanted to tell me, or why he didn't?

We took the trucks to the ops building and parked them. We would spend the next few days getting the offices set up. The next time I'd visit Samuel, would be on his fiftieth birthday as a building.

Tim Hancock

August 17-20

The next day I drove with Bailey to the operations building. Since that was where my primary office would be she wanted to get it set up first. She was doing the arranging I was only there, apparently, to carry boxes.

Hank, Ken, Ice and Shay were holding interviews in the conference room. Things were operating smoothly. Bruiser walked into my office and we stood there watching Bailey work.

"Actually spent the first night in my own bed in a long time."

"Hell. Figured you'd sleep in the bus, cause it felt right."

"Screw that, wanted me a real bed."

"You and Mandy still seein each other?"

"Yeah, had dinner last night with Ice and that Paige girl. Ya know chief, I've known Ice a long time. I ain't never seen him the way he is around her."

I caught Bailey's smile and the "I told ya so" look.

238

"Think she's good for him?"

"Hell yes, she's zactly what he needs. Treats him like a king too."

"Hey, Bailey."

"Yes, Bri."

"Maybe I'm playin favorites, how's she as a worker?"

"Good as they come, she's my right hand."

"Call her temp service, thank em for me, then make her the office manager."

"Bri, I'm the office manager."

"Oh, well, no. I meant make her the assistant office manager."

She giggled. It was cute. "Ok, boss anything you say."

"Just as long as she's here to stay."

"Say no more." Bruiser was smiling at me "What! We need all the good people we can get. Besides, your girlfriend's already full time."

Bailey and I went to lunch with Hank and Shay. They had completed interviews for the day and were going to spend the rest of the day getting their offices ready.

Hank made a good point. "Been closest thing like a regular day, since we opened this business."

Shay added, "I still jump, every time the phone rings."

The rest of the day was pretty much routine. By the end of it, the place was a regular office, ready for business. I went home,

Bailey said since she was spending so much time at my place, she was gonna go to her apartment and pack things up. I asked if she wanted help.

"Thanks Bri, I just want to be alone and think a little tonight."

Back at my place, alone, I didn't sleep well. I was worried about losing her. I resisted the urge to call her.

My phone rang just after midnight. I answered it quickly; hoping it was Bailey. It was Samuel.

"Sorry to wake you Brian. I felt the need to talk."

"Samuel I really don't need this shit right now."

"You promised you would visit."

"For Gods sake Samuel, it's only been a day. You're acting like a fucking child."

"I am not a child Brian, I have things I need to tell you. There are some things you need to know."

"Samuel, can't this wait?"

"Brian, I cannot shoulder all of this guilt, not anymore and not alone. Those things that happened, It was not me."

I cut him off. "No Samuel, it was the drugs, right?" "Goodnight Samuel."

I hung up the phone, then took it off the hook. I tried to go back to sleep. It just wasn't in the cards.

The next day I met her at the Admin building.

She wanted to get my office set up there. I was watching her put things away.

"Bailey, everything ok?"

She sat on my desk and lit a smoke. "Bri, please sit down."

I did. I felt a knot in the pit of my stomach.

"I've been doing some thinking. The fact is, I'm not done. I love you, I'm sure of that."

"I…"

"Please let me finish. I know you love me too. That should be enough, but I just. I need some time to think. Please try to understand. I lived with my dad through college. I haven't been on my own very long. We have been through a lot lately. Things happened kinda fast. I will move in, if you still want me to. I just want a few days to get my head straight." She leaned over and kissed me softly.

"Of course I still want you to move in. Only if it's what *you* want. You want the spare room?" Her smile told me I finally understood.

"I think, for now. As long as you don't mind if I have a sleep over, now and then."

"A, sleep over? Honey, you can have anyone come over anytime, it's your house too."

She giggled, stood up and kissed me on the forehead. "Silly, I meant a sleep over, in *your* room."

She left me in my office shaking my head. I felt better. A year ago I'd have never gotten that far. I would have interrupted her, pissed he off and been unhappy. Was I *finally* growing up?

We spent the rest of that day taking care of regular business. Bailey and I went to dinner with Ice and Paige. The funniest part of the evening was listening to Paige call him Stephen.

They were like a couple a teenage kids. Before we left Ice took me aside.

"Your packages will be ready Saturday."

"So we can plan on doing this Sunday?"

"Yep, kinda ironic."

"What's that?"

"Fifty years exactly, since it all happened."

"Hadn't thought about that. See you tomorrow, Stephen."

"Fuck off, Bri."

I went home alone. The house was quiet. Bailey called a few minutes after I got there.

"Just wanted to tell you goodnight."

"Glad you did."

"I left you a gift on your bed."

"What is it?" "Go look." I walked into the bedroom. There was a very large pink teddy bear, wearing my softball T-shirt.

"Very sweet."

"Thought you might get lonely."

"I love you Bailey."

"Goodnight Bri, love you too."

The phone rang again that night. I switched the ringer off. "Not tonight Samuel."

The next day, Tom paid a visit to my office.

"Hey Brian, just stopped by to pick up my things. I figured I'd stop in and say goodbye."

"We're gonna miss ya Tom."

"I'll miss you guys too."

"So, what you got planned?"

"Taking a job with the OSBI."

"Should be nice."

"Yeah, pays ok, and it mostly a desk job."

"I guess I need to write you a check, for your investment."

"Nah, Bailey already took care of it. The group bought me out. Now the eight of them own thirty."

"Tom, keep in touch."

"Count on it Brian, you guys are still my friends. If you ever need anything, you got a contact in the State Bureau now."

"Thanks Tom, might come in handy."

"Brian, what are you gonna do, about that building?"

"Got a good plan for it Tom, you might not want to know. After Sunday, it won't be a problem."

"I'll use some influence, and keep the area clear." "Thanks again. Tom, if you got time, bring the wife by the house sometime."

"Count on it man."

 I called everyone to see what his or her weekend plans were. I wanted to set up another

Saturday pool party.

Ken and Gunner were taking their wives to
Kansas City for the weekend.

Ice said he'd like to be there, but he'd have
to check with Paige. He got back to me quickly
they were coming.

Hank and Shay confirmed immediately. Bruiser
and Mandy were coming too. I went to Bailey's
to invite her personally.

She looked up form her work and smiled. I
realized it was the first time I'd seen her
that day.

"Hi boss."

"Hey doll. You busy Saturday?"

"Might have a hot date."

She was joking, but my heart still skipped a
beat.

"Nothing planned."

"You want to come by, having a get together.
Pool thing. Gonna try to do it a few times,
before the summer's over."

"We might be a little tired."

"How come?"

She smiled. "I was hoping to move my stuff
Friday after work."

"No problem, we'll close up early, right after
your girls get payroll done, and I'll get
help."

She stood and her hands behind my neck. "Why
Mr. Kelly, I get the impression you missed
me."

I put my arms around her and kissed her. "The bears ok, but not much for conversation. Not much of a kisser either.

Bailey left early to finish packing. I finished my work for the day feeling happy. Soon our lives would be normal. My first though was back to normal, but they had never been normal. When Samuel called this time, I hadn't gotten to bed yet.

"Brian, why are you avoiding me?"

"Samuel, you are starting to sound like a jealous girlfriend. I'm *not* avoiding you. I *am* busy."

"Brian, I need you to know, you were wrong. The drugs did change me. I did some horrible things. I am not very proud of myself. I am not trying to make excuses. "The experiment made everything different."

"I'm sure it did. It left you as part of a fuckin building, and alone."

"I wasn't alone. There were lots of others there."

"Yes, and you forced them into your makeshift furnace."

"Of course, you would think that."

"What the fuck else would I think. That's what the fuck happened. I'm not going to let you absolve yourself with me Samuel. Get a fuckin Priest for that." I hung up again.

"This motherfucker thinks you're his friend Bri." "Fine, but my friends don't call this late". "Fuck em."

I spent the next morning recruiting movers.

Hank and Shay knew before I did and it was in their day-planers. Bruiser and Ice said they'd help too. All of the girls from admin had already volunteered.

It didn't take long. Most of her furniture she gave away. What little was left we put in storage. The girls helped her put stuff away and us guys carried boxes. My house was starting to look like a woman lived there. I was feeling warm and fuzzy.

The best way to describe the guestroom, was definitely a typical teenage girl' room. It looked a lot like my sisters' room, when we were growing up. All it was missing was the teen-beat posters. They had been replaced by some very pricey lookin paintings. She was making herself at home.

After everyone left, Bailey made a nice dinner. We ate in the Den.

"Bri, I don't want you to think I'm taking over. If I change anything that bothers you, tell me."

"Bailey, this is your house too now. Change anything you like. Other than this room, I haven't changed much of anything in this house since I bought it."

"Are you sure?"

"Darlin' I like what you've done already."

"You get this room Bri. I won't change a thing in here. You get your room too of course, for now. I will ask, before I do anything too drastic."

"Don't worry Bailey, as long as you are in the

room, it will work fine for me."

We watched TV for a while then went to bed, much to my disappointment, in different rooms.

The next morning you could tell she felt at home. She was getting things ready for the party. I couldn't do a thing.

"I'm the hostess now baby, officially, so this party reflects on me. You get the grill and the pool ready and I'll let you know if I need anything." I did as I was told.

Our guests showed up on time. The guys were told to go out by the pool. We were ok with that. We were sitting in lounge chairs, having a few beers. Hank surprised us all.

"Guys I want you all to know. I'm gonna be a Daddy!"

"Holy hell, you shittin me?"

"No, I swear. We knew yesterday for sure. Well, at least that's when I found out. Shay's known for awhile I guess."

"Hank, if I'd known, I'd never let her…"

"She knew that too, part of the reason she didn't tell us."

"I'm happy for you Hank, both a ya."

"Thanks Bruiser."

"Yeah, man me too."

"Sure Ice. Chief, somethin wrong?"

"Hell no, I'm happy as hell for ya. Bailey know?"

"You know how those two are."

"Yeah, I do."

"Guess you guys are gonna need a bigger place."

"As a matter of fact, that's the other thing." "Reason we were late is cause we were lookin at the house next door."

"That'll be great Hank, but we'll never be able to keep those two apart, not that I'd ever really want to. Congratulations, I really am happy for you."

"Good, cause I have a question for you. Bailey doesn't know this part yet. Will you be my best man."

That part shocked me, the two of them had sworn they would never get married. Guess a kid'll change things.

"Like you even needed to ask."

"Ok, keep that part quiet, we're gonna announce it later."

"Our lips are sealed."

The girls joined us on the patio, a little later. They were ready for the pool and all looked good. Bailey was in a new blue one piece, like everything else, it looked good on her.

Hank and Shay made the official announcement, while we ate. I acted surprised, Bailey truly was. Shay asked her to be her maid of honor, Hank asked me again, for the first time, to be his best man.

It was a real good day, everyone was happy. After everyone left, Bailey and I took separate showers and met in the living room. We talked cuddled up on the couch.

"I knew about the baby. I never expected the wedding part."

"They both caught me off guard."

"Shay wanted to wait to tell everyone, until we were out of the building. She didn't want to be left out again."

"Bailey, if she had lost the baby, I couldn't have lived with that."

"I know honey, I wanted her to tell you. I *should* have told you. I felt like I had betrayed you. That's why I." "I promise I'll never keep anything from you again."

"You did the right thing Bailey. She needed to trust you."

"I'm glad nothing happened."

"I'm so glad you didn't have to let her down."

"I love you, Bri."

"I love you too."

That night we slept in her room. I felt like I shouldn't have been there. It really did feel like, a teenage girl's room. I was happy to be with her.

August 21

The guys and I met at the building. It was time to finish it. Ice was putting the finishing touches on his packages.

"What's the menu Ice?"

"Well you got your basic C-4 with remote detonation. These small ones are for the garages, five for the big one, four for the small one."

"Should be enough to turn them to sand."

"The bigger ones need to be placed through-out the building. The biggest one needs to, well, go in the hole."

"Ok, where do we need to put em."

"He pulled out a makeshift map. I marked all the spots."

We all studied it for awhile.

Hank said, "You know this is gonna piss him off."

"I figure it will."

"Should be a lot of fun."

"Should be the worst yet."

"Best get it over then."

We started in the Main building, upstairs. We were placing one of Ices' packages in each room. We had barely gotten started, when the phone rang. *I hate to disappoint you Samuel, but I don't have time to talk."* We let it ring and continued. We had to put them in the corners of the four corner offices. Evidently, he hadn't figured it out yet.

We finished the upstairs and started down. The phone was still ringing. We quickly placed eight packages along the walls in the pool and two in the center of the room.

"Ok now the bay."

The phone upstairs continued to ring.

The phone in the hole was ringing too.

"Let's get the back wall first. Then we can toss one in each cage. The hole last."

"Brian, what are you doing?"

Samuel's' voice seemed to be coming from everywhere.

"Shit," Bruiser swore.

"How in the hell?"

"Easy Hank. Just putting out some poison Samuel."

"I do not have mice, Brian. I ask again, what are you doing."

"Truth is Samuel, I have decided to change our agreement."

"What do you mean?"

"I have to stop you Samuel."

"Stop me! You can't stop me."

"I will stop you."

We kept working while I talked.

"They tried to burn me Brian It won't work."

"I don't want to burn you Samuel."

"What then? Explosives! I can't let you do it. Brian you bastard."

We had all of the bombs set, except the hole. I walked to it. As I bent to throw it in the top step moved. As I fell, I heard the doors close behind me. Then everything went black.

It quickly started to warm up. I yelled through the door.

"Ice can you hear me."

"We hear ya chief," Hank answered. "Ice went for the torch"

"When he gets back, you and Bruiser get the rest of those charges set, in the garages."

"I ain't leaving you chief."

"Damn it Hank, you have to do this. If he can't get me out, blow this bastard to hell."

"Chief."

"I mean it, do it."

"You mean to kill me Brian?"

"I mean to end this, all of it."

"But, I don't want to die." It was getting hotter.

"Samuel, think about what you did. Think about

all the innocent lives you wasted."

"Don't you see, it wasn't just me. There were lots of people in here Brian. All of us were stuck in here together. They are all quiet now. Now, it's just me. There were patients in here too. They were responsible for the worst of it."

I walked to the center of the hole and sat the package down.

"I don't believe you this time Samuel. I think you've been in control all along. I think you are such a sick, barbaric fuck, you got off on it. Finally, the others quit trying. Gave up, so to speak."

"No your wrong there's still another in…" The voiced changed. "Such an asshole."

It was getting hot faster. I could hear Ice with the torch.

"Who are you?"

"Who I am isn't fucking important, Bri. The fact is you will never get out of here. Now, you should worry about that."

"Ice, how's it coming with door?"

"I can't fucking cut it chief."

"Fuck it Ice, get the fuck out. Blow this fucker."

"I can't do that chief. I would never be able to forgive myself. Neither would Bailey. Think about it chief, see fuckin needs you. If you die saving him, Shawn will never let me live it down."

"It ain't gonna matter in fifteen minutes I'll

be a roast."

"Guess I got fifteen minutes then."

"Did they get the other stuff set?"

"Yeah," it was Hank. "It's all set to go."

"Then go do it."

"Sorry chief, I made a promise to my cousin, gotta bring ya back."

"They will never get the fucking doors open, you're fucking finished, Brian."

"So are you dick head."

"So be it."

He turned up the heat. The entire building started to shake.

"Hank, it's over Go NOW!" I heard Bruiser.

"He's right we gotta go now." I heard them leaving.

Hank yelled through the door. "Ten minutes, get the hell out of there." Then he was gone.

"Guess it's just you and me asshole."

"Brian," I heard Samuel whisper in my ear, "There's a tunnel, to the garage. I tried to tell you it has never been just me. He was a patient, he's always been stronger than me." The angry voice was on the outside.

"You and me we fucking go together. Your friends will suffer Brian, more than you or me, I fucking win."

"Brian, his name is Matthew Henderson. He is the one that brought them all here, and did that horrible thing. I could not stop him."

"Matthew, you fucking pussy."

"How the fuck? That little shit Samuel, how did he tell you?"

I was moving toward the end of the hall.

"Behind the bookshelf Brian. I can help you get out of here, but you must go now."

I slammed the shelf to the side. The tunnel was there.

"Samuel, you son of a bitch, you fucking bastard, you let him go.

"Yes, I did." Now both voices were in the open "I made my mistakes with you Matthew. Now I have to set things right."

"It's too fucking late, He will never make it out in time."

I had five minutes. I dove into the tunnel. I could hear the arguing as I crawled towards the garage.

"Sammy, you picked a hell of a time to become a wimp."

"Don't call me that Matthew. I hate Sammy. I am not being a wimp. I will not let you hurt anyone again. Even if I have to die."

"At least he goes with us, I'll have that."

I was in the larger garage. The lights on the bombs were green.

"Brian take the ambulance, he has no control."

I started the car, and crashed through the door. I had just cleared the building when the first of the bombs went off. The blast caused me to temporally lose control. I got the car

headed back in the right direction and made for the gate.

The next explosion lifted the back of the ambulance up, but also pushed it forward faster. I was clear of the gate, when the main building went. I turned left and drove the half-mile to where the others were waiting.

The Police had the road blocked there. I pulled in next to Ice's truck. I was glad to see them. They all embraced me.

"Hey guys, I survived that, don't kill me now." Everyone laughed.

We waited about an hour and went back to check. There was a big crater where the building had been. Even the parking lot was gone. It was going to take a hell of a lot of solid fill, before it would be used again. My Ramcharger was gone too.

"Ice, I think you used enough."

He clapped me on the back laughing. "Hell, could have done it with about half, maybe even less"

"Let's go home."

I drove the ambulance back to my house. It had saved my life and I was going to see it restored, it looked like shit now. Bailey met me at the door.

"Is it over?"

"I kissed her passionately, "yes love, it's over."

"Bri, is it safe to have that here?"

I nodded. "They were in the building.

Everything else was a just tool. Believe me when I tell you I think we have heard the last of it."

We went into the house. I took a shower washing the day away. I was tired but it was finally over. We could get on with our lives.

Bailey and I went to bed together that night, and it was different. There had been a tension between us, the pull of the building. It was gone now. We started out just kind of horsing around. Mostly we were playing and then she started with the tickling. Before long we were kissing. Eventually, things started to heat up. We made love slowly and gently. After all it was the first time.

Epilogue July 21 Present

It really was over. The building destroyed. We have all been to the place several times. That's all it is now, a location. It's not going to be that for long.

I was contacted by a very large religious organization. They offered me a huge sum for the spot. Normally, with any church group, I would have just let them have it. I was pretty familiar with this particular group, anyone in this area is. Their offer was more than fair, but I told them the offer wasn't quite high enough. Within two weeks they doubled it. Seems the good Lord had been especially good to their shepherd. He spared his life, when he didn't reach the mandated four million, a few years back.

Now maybe it's wrong of me to be so judgmental, but I know the history. I plan to put the money to good use. Half will go to fund a school for under privileged kids. The rest will go to the Oklahoma City Bombing and 9/11 memorial funds.

A few weeks after the end, we broke ground on

the Headquarters building. Hank and Shay Got
married and named their son Samuel. They have
two more now. Hank is the head of our Oklahoma
City operation. He got pretty old and gray
that last day. He said the thought of me
blowing up put twenty years on him. Shay is
taking time off to be with the kids.

Bailey and I got married too, six months
later. We have a little girl. She's due to
have our second any day. We spend our time
mostly here at the headquarters building. She
wanted to keep working. I didn't even try to
argue. Well I'm not stupid, am I?

Ice dated Paige for six years before they
finally got serious enough to make it
official. They are hoping to have their first
child soon. Ice runs the operations department
of our Tulsa division. Paige is the Human
resources director for Kelly Security Inc.
Poor thing; she still works for Bailey.

Gunner was with us for a few more years and
retired. He is still in the area and still a
member of the board of directors for Kelly
Corp.

Ken moved back to Florida after his wife died.
He sold his interest in the company back to
me. He bought himself a boat, bigger than
mine, with the money he got. We go to visit
once a year. He takes us out on the boat and
we fish. Just like he said to me back in the
bay that day. He spends most of his time
fishing and annoying his grand kids. He's got
a great life, if you ask me.

 Shawn was fine when he came back. He went
back to school, at the University of Oklahoma

and got his degree in Criminal Justice. He is
now the Director of our Investigations
Division. That was something I never planned
on. When he brought the Idea to me, I said yes
right away. I don't regret that decision. He
hasn't married anyone yet. I have heard that
he's got a thing for one of the girls in the
accounting office.

Bruiser and Mandy are still living together.
They say they don't plan to ever get married
or have kids. Bruiser opened our new office in
Kansas City. It's our biggest operating center
yet. They were working out of a temporary
office up there and already had clients
standing in line. He is back here now mostly
to lead a new division. Sometimes security
isn't enough. He is taking over the personal
protective service division.

Tom served the OSBI faithfully. He was killed
in the line of duty at the Alfred P. Murrah
Federal Building, April 19, 1995. There is a
plaque in the lobby, near the ambulance
remembering him.

Now and then I'll hear a story about how some
old desk or file cabinet does something weird.
I have to laugh. I haven't heard of anyone
getting hurt by it. I can't help but think
maybe one of those other people, the quiet
ones, got in the furniture to hide. Maybe he
banished them there. I can only guess. There
really is no way to know, is there? When I
hear about these things, I send someone to buy
the troublesome item. Often, they have already
been destroyed. When we do get them, after we
confirm it came from the building, we put it
in an old warehouse. We have a hell of a lot

of stuff there now. I figure it's only fair. Knowing what little I do know.

I had the ambulance restored. I parked it in the lobby of this building the day we opened it. Had Custom plates made for it too, Samuel 21.

Now don't be surprised, if you come in the building some day. You just might see me sitting in that old ambulance. The one in the lobby, painted to look like one of our patrol cars, talking to myself. I never break a promise

A-21

Made in the USA
San Bernardino, CA
04 July 2013